HEATWAVE

Also by Abbie Amy

Daughter of Wednesday
Ink for Two

Heatwave

Abbie Amy

For Jeff

JONI

I first saw her in the grocery line. She worked
there after school and on some weekends—more
often during the summer. Everyone called her Etta
and the name suited her. I remember thinking that she
looked nice out of school uniform. She wore a cream
cardigan with a sunflower stitched on it under a teal
apron. Somehow the cardigan wasn't dirty. She must
have been magic.

The fairy lights in the store were strung
lopsidedly along the walls. They flashed crimson
and blue as I waited in the checkout line with my
dad. I loved Christmas, even the wonky plastic tree

decorated with tinsel in the corner of the store. Mum said we were a strictly no tinsel family, favouring white and glass ornaments with gold fairy lights. Dad liked tinsel, though. He would sneak bags of it in the house and Ellie and I would help him put it on the tree. Mum always shook her head at it and joked that Christmas was cancelled. Christmas was good for us. Mum drank too much wine and Dad didn't reprimand her for it like he usually did. Ellie and I would watch movies together until the early hours of the morning, Mum's snoring lofting in the background. It was the one time my family could pretend that we all got along.

The next trolley rolled up to the counter and we all shuffled forward. It was Jamie Akerman and his mum. Earlier they had nearly run me down with their trolley in a rush to get their shopping done. Jamie was popular in the good way. He was liked by everyone: peers and teachers. He was also very attractive, with soft eyes that seemed to invite you in and long arms that I imagined would feel safe to be wrapped around. Half the girls on my volleyball team had a crush on him. I found this made it harder to speak to him, though we went to the same parties and sat at the same table at lunch.

At the counter, Jamie eyed Etta in an appraising

way, his cheeks slightly flushed. I caught myself thinking that they would make an attractive couple—Etta's curly blonde hair and Jamie's freckles. Etta gazed up at Jamie through her eyelashes as she pressed the buttons on the till. She was bashful but in the alluring way. Jamie's entire body leant towards her. You wouldn't have guessed that she was in the year below and generally known for being shy. I watched with a strange feeling in my stomach as words danced out of her mouth and Jamie smiled back. They were completely drawn to each other. Then Etta whipped around to the next customer and Jamie continued to stare at her. She couldn't see it, but I could. The strange look on his face—like he wanted more.

Dad squeezed my shoulder and I wheeled the trolley forward and began to put our items on the counter. The beeping of the scanner blended in with the background drawling of "Santa Baby". I watched as Etta served Michael Holland. Etta spoke easily to Michael, even though he lived on the outskirts of Cedar Valley and avoided most of the town. But Etta had a way of drawing conversation out of people—even the tough ones like Michael. I envied that. I needed a plan for everything. I had to go over what I wanted to say in my head a hundred times before

I said it. She was a field of wildflowers growing in multicoloured flurries and I was the curated bouquet trimmed at the florist and presented with wrapping paper and a generic card.

Michael gave Etta a rare smile as he pushed his trolley through the doors. I stared at my shoes as Etta greeted us and began scanning our items. She asked my dad how his day had been.

"Same old," he said.

Etta gave him an understanding smile. "Mine, too. It's good to know things don't change as you get older." Dad laughed at that.

I liked the way she packed our bags, putting the heavy items at the bottom and the eggs on top. "You used to be on the volleyball team," observed Etta.

Dad raised his eyebrows, the lines in his forehead deepening as he did. "Correct," he said. "Long time ago now."

"My dad says you were the best the team had. There hasn't been anyone as good as you since."

"He's exaggerating," Dad laughed. He got this a lot.

"Do you still play?" Etta asked, a light in her eyes.

Dad paused then shook his head. "I have bills to pay and mouths to feed now." I looked down, tucking my hair behind my ears. "Responsibilities take choices away from you."

Etta nodded and punched the card machine, offering it to Dad. "Well, here's hoping you can play again soon." Dad paid, the machine omitting a beeping noise, and grabbed our bags. I took one from him. "Happy Christmas!" Etta called as we made our way to the door. I smiled at her as best I could, but it felt like more of a grimace, and followed Dad to the carpark.

"Mum," I tried again. No response. I pressed my back against the wall and sighed. I had spent most of the Christmas break outside her bedroom door, pleading to the wood. Occasionally there'd be a shuffling sound or the light would flick on, momentarily casting a warm glow beneath the door. Then it would be snuffed out with a harsh click.

"Please, Mum," I repeated, though not loud enough for her to hear. "He isn't coming back."

Cedar Valley was not a large town. Everyone knew everyone and so everyone knew everyone's business. The news would have spread by now: Leonard Fraser had finally left his wife and two kids on Boxing Day.

My dad was gone. Christmas was the one time we pretended to be happy and he had played along for the last time. There was no goodbye, no tearful pleas. He was gone in the morning before I woke up.

My mum hadn't left her room since. Ellie had booked an overseas trip without a return ticket. And all I could think about was the large photography book of sailing on the kitchen counter. I had bought it for him for Christmas. He'd been so excited to open it that he had torn through the dust jacket in his eagerness to reveal what was under the dancing penguin paper I had picked out. He had said he loved the present. So why did he leave it behind?

I knocked on the door a little harder. "Do you want me to make you some lunch?" Footsteps thundered on the stairs and Ellie appeared with a flushed face and wearing her cream puffer jacket. In her hands was a brown paper bag. She'd gone out earlier to buy the mini bottles of shampoo and soap from the pharmacy before her flight tomorrow morning.

Ellie looked at me and then to Mum's door. She clicked her tongue. "Don't waste your time waiting for something to come back that doesn't want to be here."

"I know Dad's not coming back," I said with an

edge to my voice. I recrossed my legs but didn't get up.

Ellie's eyes hardened. "I didn't mean Dad."

I stared in silence as she trotted down to her room and slammed the door. I'd been close with Ellie growing up. We used to ride our bikes around Cedar and build pillow forts in the living room. Then I joined the volleyball team and Ellie performed in every theatre production our school put on. We became different people, and while I still wanted to be friends, Ellie was no longer interested.

I stayed outside Mum's room until I was covered in shadows and stiff from sitting so long. Ellie told me not to waste my time. But she was leaving and I was going to be the one left with the pieces. This was my problem now.

I drove Ellie to the airport the next day. Mum stayed in her room the entire morning.

I wanted to park and walk Ellie to security but she insisted that the drop off was fine. I waited as she opened the door and got her bags. For a moment I thought she was going to walk off without a final goodbye. But she stuck her head through the open passenger window and looked me dead in the eye.

"Do something fun this summer," she said. I laughed and ran my hands up and down the steering wheel, my knuckles white from clutching it. "I mean it," Ellie insisted. "Get through the school year and then party all summer with your friends."

I nodded, a sudden lump in my throat that made it impossible to speak. A car behind me honked. I wasn't meant to be parked in the drop off zone. "You have fun too," I managed, my voice strangled.

Then my sister was gone. She walked through the doors without looking back.

With Ellie away, the house was still. I cooked and cleaned and tried not to think about Dad. The weeks and months passed in a strange kaleidoscope of shapes and moments—some blurred and distant and others so sharp they hurt to think about.

At school I hid in my English classroom whenever I could. Everyone knew what had happened, and while the girls on my volleyball team rubbed my arm and hugged me and told me I could talk to them, the invitation expired after a week. I was expected to return to the usual Joni. So I hid from them. And I cried. Or I tried calling Ellie but she never answered.

I saw Etta a lot during school. She took advanced biology a year early. I had done the same thing. I felt like that connected us somehow. I mostly spotted her in hallways or with her friend, Skye Matthews. And of course, I saw her the night of the dance.

The dance was one memory from the past school year that stuck out so vividly compared to the murky blur of all the other weeks. Then summer began in gentle heat and crickets singing in the evening. I started to think I had dreamt the events of that night until one day late July, where the heatwave broke in a thunderstorm and pouring rain—and I saw him again.

I liked being at the mall. I liked the too-bright fluorescent lighting and the unenthusiastic background music and the constant recycled air that dried out my skin. I had spent most of the summer milling around the shops and buying things I didn't need. It was a relief to be alone in a crowd of people.

I sat outside the ice cream parlour at a white stone table underneath the turquoise striped umbrellas. Some of the kids from school worked there, but today it was just a girl in her twenties with a dull look in her eyes. She'd barely glanced at me as I'd paid and only shrugged when I told her to keep the change.

I sipped a vanilla milkshake, watching as a mum only a few years older than myself struggled to get her two children to sit down and eat the ice cream dripping from the cones onto their fingers. I wondered if it had been like that for my mum—fussing over two daughters fourteen months apart before she was twenty. She never went to university—never partied the way most did in their twenties. I was certain she resented us for it, especially now.

My watch told me I had been at the mall six hours. Sipping the rest of my milkshake, I kicked the metal chair backwards and took one last look at the mum and her children. She was ignoring them now, scrolling through her phone while they stuck their tiny fingers into their ice cream and licked them clean.

I carried my bags of shopping out of the sparkling mall and into the carpark. The spell broke.

When I had arrived at the mall the sky had been bright blue. Now, it was overcast with angry black clouds clustering together. The forecast was for late rain but it looked as if the storm was coming early. Cedar always endured an annual heatwave, usually in June. This one had come later.

In the car I turned on the engine and waited for the air conditioning to start. I let my eyes flutter closed as the car shuddered into life. Mum was going to Jacky's house for dinner and endless bottles of wine. She would end up staying the night there. She'd been doing that a lot since summer started, but at least it was better than locking herself in her room and drinking alone.

I heard the rain before I opened my eyes. Tiny drops in an uneven beat spread across the windscreen. Then the downpour came. I watched as the outside world dissolved into a waterfall from the safety of my car. The rain was so heavy I almost missed him.

He stood staring up at the sky, one hand on his bike that was locked up behind the shops. He was already soaked but didn't seem to care and didn't appear to be in a hurry to get out of the rain. My hand was at the ignition before I knew what I was doing. I pulled up beside him—he still hadn't turned to me— and rolled down the window.

"Jamie!" I called out, having to strain my voice to be heard over the rain.

Jamie Akerman, popular in all the good ways, turned at the sound of my voice, which had somehow carried across the storm. He was dressed in what must have been beige shorts and a white t-shirt, both now soaked and clinging to his body. Water drenched his usually curly hair. His chest heaved as he took in the storm. Jamie's eyes flashed as he recognised me then his face split into a grin.

Who did he recognise me as? The quiet Joni who sat at his table while he commanded the conversation by a single look? Or the Joni from the night of the dance whose lips he leant towards?

Jamie threw his palms out to the sky and spun around. I shook my head in astonishment. "Isn't this amazing?" he called back. A clap of thunder threatened in the background. I flinched.

"Get in," I shouted. "I'll drive you home."

"I have my bike," he said. "I can just ride."

I nearly laughed. "No car will be able to see you in this!"

Jamie didn't reply. Another growl of thunder rolled over, and it sounded closer this time. I saw a bolt of lightning in the distance. "Get in the car," I repeated. My anxiety must have showed in my voice because his eyes changed and his eyebrows lifted, and then he opened the car door and shuffled inside. "What about your bike?" I said when the door closed.

"Oh. Yeah I better get that." I waited as Jamie sprinted outside and chucked his bike into the massive boot.

"Where's your house?" I asked once he was back in the car, rolling up my window and shutting off the thunderous noise of the rain hitting the pavement. I realised that my arms were wet from the splashes that came through the window.

"Behind the school," replied Jamie. His hair was dripping and it looked as if rain had soaked through his shoes. I shivered. I hated cold feet. "But I can't go there."

I cocked my head. "Why not?"

He grimaced. "My sister's having a party and I don't feel like dealing with drunk people right now." That surprised me but I kept the thought to myself. "Why are you hiding out at the mall? Isn't Paige having a girls only gathering or some shit like that today?" I shook my head. I had no idea about a gathering. Jamie took my response as a no. "Fair enough," he said. "You'd probably have more fun here anyway."

I nodded as there was a sudden lump in my throat. It wasn't that I wanted to spend time with those girls but it reminded me of how alone I truly was.

"Are you okay?" Jamie cocked his head at me, his brows pulled together.

His words echoed in my head. I couldn't

remember the last time someone had asked me that. I said, "I used to hate it when Ellie had parties in the summer."

Jamie blinked, startled by the change in subject. "Who?"

"My sister," I said. "She's away for the summer—longer maybe. I took her to the airport. She's probably island hopping right now on some millionaire's yacht. Or maybe she's dancing past midnight in a city that keeps the skylights on all night. I don't know. She's having the time of her life—"

I stopped when I noticed Jamie had been silent for the entire time I had been speaking. He stared at me, right at me, with a look on his face I couldn't place. "What?" I said, tugging at the ends of my hair.

Jamie shrugged. "I don't think I've ever heard you talk that much. Ever."

Outside, the rain eased slightly and I saw that my windscreen wipers were able to do their job. "I do talk," I said, digging my nails into the steering wheel. The truth was that I wanted to talk to Jamie because he had asked me if I was okay—not told me that I was going to be. He had cared, even just in that moment, about how I felt. The night of the dance plummeted into my vision. The shadows on the carpet. The broken girl in an emerald dress. My face damp with tears. Jamie there, listening. I talked the night of the dance.

"I do talk," I repeated. "Most of the time people aren't listening to me." I put the car into drive before he could respond. Without looking over at him, I drove out of the carpark and took us towards my house. Where else were we going to go?

We were both quiet on the five-minute journey to my house. I was grateful. Concentrating on driving helped soothe the jitters running through my restless legs. At my house, Jamie got out of the car and followed me inside.

"Do you want a drink?" I asked, letting him step into the hall and locking the door behind us. I led him through the entranceway and into the kitchen. Jamie followed after taking off his shoes—even though I hadn't asked him to. His eyes darted around the house, pausing on the crystal chandelier in the hallway Mum had insisted on, and then resting on the enormous TV Dad had insisted on.

I opened the fridge and pulled out a can of lemonade. He thanked me and popped it open with the small fizzing sound as the air released. While he sipped, I poured myself cherry cordial and nodded towards the sofas in the living room just across from us.

"I didn't know you were rich," observed Jamie bluntly. "You're never coming over to mine, you'll think it's the guest house or something."

"We're not rich," I said, a little self-consciously, although I knew he was making a joke.

"You have one of those taps that does boiling water," he said, pointing at the sink.

"My grandma bought us this house," I insisted. "She put that in."

"Okay," said Jamie, backing down. He sat on one of the white sofas and placed his lemonade on the glass coffee table. I couldn't sit yet—there was too much energy swirling inside of me ready to burst. I was coming to terms with the fact that I had invited a boy over without much thought to it.

"Do you want to change?" I blurted out. He raised an eyebrow. "I mean because your clothes are wet," I added. My heart pounded.

"I'm good," he said. "But thanks." He cleared his throat. "Are you—er…going to sit down?"

My cheeks warmed. "Okay," I said and sat in the spot farthest from him.

We looked anywhere but at each other. Jamie's face was fixed on the shelf of framed family photos. There had been one of Dad playing volleyball as a teenager but that had vanished. I suspected that Mum had removed it along with her wedding photos. My favourite one of me and Ellie on our bikes was also missing. Dad loved that photo, Ellie too. It captured me sat on my bike with my hands gripping the handlebars. There was a determined look on my face. Ellie's head was thrown back with laughter.

We were outside of Grandma's house. We'd gone there a lot when we were little and our parents were fighting. She would cook us Chicken Adobo— the smell of vinegar thick in the air as it bubbled over the stove—and reminisce about her days in the Philippines and when she might return. Mum said she would never return. She didn't like to talk about her heritage, although it was written all over her face. I'd inherited Mum's light brown skin and dark hair and eyes—also the way her mouth turned down when she was unhappy or her tendency to be upset about something but not say anything.

Jamie coughed. "Do you ever think about the dance?" He scratched his head.

"The dance?" I repeated. He nodded. My eyes fluttered closed. I saw Lyn this time, looking over my new dress with disdain, pointing out that I had forgotten to take the tag off. I saw Jamie dressed in deep blue—the kind that was almost black. And I saw that sad, beautiful girl with her hair pinned back, one curl falling loose, mouthing, *What the fuck?*

I opened my eyes. Jamie sat on the edge of the sofa, his knees bouncing up and down. "Yeah," I said. "I'm sorry about that." I tucked my hair behind my ears then folded and refolded my hands in my lap.

"It definitely wasn't your fault," he said.

"I didn't know that you and—"

"We weren't," he cut in. He rubbed a hand at the back of his neck. "Nothing official. Just friends. Well used to be. Either way…it's not your fault. I'm sorry." He was uncomfortable. I was, too. I thought about the dance even less than I thought about the day Dad left.

"Do you mind if I light some candles?" I asked. He blinked in confusion. I needed to do something with my hands; I needed to distract myself.

"Sure," he said, and I ran into the kitchen. "Are they scented?" he asked when I returned with some matches. He screwed up his face. "My sisters are obsessed with scented candles, Mum too. The house smells permanently like vanilla or caramel or something. It's nice but just a bit much." I pulled my favourite candle from the mantlepiece and stuck it in his face to smell. He leant forward. "That's actually nice," he said. He looked up at me and I felt frozen.

"What is it?"

"It's called Oceania," I said. I put the candle on the coffee table and pulled out a match. "It smells like being on holiday at the beach," I said. "Balmy summer evenings, salt water, sleeping easy. My Grandma has a house on the cliffs that overlooks the sea. I loved going there as a kid but we haven't been back much recently—" The candle was burning now, the flame flickering tentatively as the wicker crackled and the wax warmed. I turned to him. His gaze was pinned to me again. "I sleep better by the sea," I explained, then sat down closer to him.

The clock in the kitchen ticked. The rain bounced off the windows. The thunder had ceased. There was only the occasional flash of lightning through the curtains. Jamie's clothes still clung to his body and this close I could see the lines of his chest underneath. I swallowed. "Are you sure you don't want to change?" I asked for the second time. "One of Ellie's boyfriends left some of his stuff here when they broke up. I don't think he's coming back for it—it was a bad breakup—so you're okay to borrow it." He didn't look away from me. I shifted my gaze, cheeks burning with embarrassment.

Jamie suddenly rose to his feet. I thought he was going to leave and I was disappointed and relieved at the same time. He didn't leave, though. He walked in my direction and sat down next to me on the sofa. I didn't dare breathe. Jamie slipped his hand behind my neck. "Is this okay?" he asked.

"Yes," I barely whispered and Jamie's lips came down to meet mine.

He was soft at first, asking the questions and waiting for my answers. His lips tasted faintly of toffee. Light stubble grazed my chin. I reached for him and my hands found his damp t-shirt. I gripped it like he was gravity.

Jamie gave out a low moan in the back of his throat and I couldn't believe that it was me who had done that to him. I pushed him back onto the sofa and hitched my legs on either side of him. He gripped me and the kissing became hungry, desperate, as if we both needed the distraction. I pulled his t-shirt up and over his head. Skin. So much of his skin beneath me. I wanted it. I wanted to wear it and hold it and be owned by it.

Jamie breathed heavily. "Have you?" he asked.

"No," I exhaled. "Never. You?"

He shook his head. It surprised me.

"Should we go to my room?" I suggested.

"Is that what you want?"

More than anything.

"Yes," I said and I rolled gently off him.

I led him upstairs to my bedroom. We stayed there until the rain stopped, the sun trying and failing to peak out from the grey July sky.

It didn't stop with that one night. I told no one about what we were doing. I desperately wanted to confide in someone but I had the prickly feeling that if I did then it would suddenly be over. I also had no one to confide in. I had friends at school—people to sit with at lunch and drink with at parties. But I didn't have someone I could trust my secrets to.

We always met at my house because it was empty. Mum hadn't returned but had left slurred messages on my voicemail in the early hours of the morning. Jamie would come over with his dark eyes and trainers and his hands reaching for me before I'd even closed the door. Sometimes we were naked before we'd reached my bedroom. After, I would go searching through the house for our clothes as if I had someone who cared that I was undressing a boy on the stairs.

Jamie didn't like to talk about himself so he asked questions about me. And I told him. The more I spoke, the more I was filled with colours I had never seen before. He listened to every word and thought I confessed—and at the end of it he still wanted more. I felt as if there was someone who cared about me, Joni. I didn't want the summer to end.

My head rested in the crook of his arm. We were on our backs, lying on top of my bed after an afternoon in the pool. Jamie's long legs stretched before me. I stared down at our feet as they rubbed together. My wet hair clung to my neck. Jamie told me he wanted to hear me talk about the beach again.

"Why?" I laughed.

"Because you have candles that smell like it and shells in every corner of your room and you seem lighter when you talk about the ocean." I turned my head to look up at him. He had freckles across his nose, very light ones, that no one saw until they were this close. I thought about how many people had seen Jamie's freckles. "Come on," Jamie said and nudged me back into the present. "I want to hear about the beach."

So I told Jamie how Mum and Dad would drive us down to the beach house to stay with Grandma. I told him how we would go orca watching and explore the rock pools and fall asleep with sand between our toes. Ellie had dad's complexion so she was always getting sunburnt on her nose while my skin turned golden. I could recall how the air tasted of salt. I told him how I felt safe at the beach.

I didn't tell him how his steady presence also made me feel safe, his hands brushing over me like the lapping of waves. This summer had been lonely before the storm; the echoes of my family were in every corner of the house. But, like ghosts, I couldn't catch them. Maybe Jamie would become one of those shadows? My heart plummeted at the thought.

"Are you okay?" came Jamie's voice. My eyes stung and a warm tear rolled down my cheek onto the slope of my nose. I wiped my eyes with the back of my hand.

"I'm fine," I managed but the tears wouldn't stop. Suddenly I was sobbing and trying to push Jamie away so I could get out of bed and away from him but he wouldn't let me. He pulled me into him, my head on his lap. Jamie clung onto me until I succumbed and cried, my chest heaving. Eventually I fell asleep from the sun and the exhaustion.

The next day Jamie turned up at my house with a gift bag. "What's that?" I asked as I let him inside. We walked into the kitchen and he perched himself on one of the bar stools.

"Go ahead and open it," he said with an annoying smile.

"What is it?" I repeated and he rolled his eyes at me.

"Just open it," he implored.

I narrowed my eyes but ruffled through the tissue paper until I dug up what was inside. "Do you like it?" Jamie asked, his voice unsteady. I stared down at what was in my hands. It was a delicate clay orca painted black and white attached to a silver chain. I turned it over in my fingers and the orca had my name on the belly. A warmth spread through my body. "My sister makes them," Jamie explained. "She has her own jewellery business."

I opened my mouth then closed it. Opened it and closed it. "You didn't have to get me anything," I managed to say.

"I know I didn't have to," said Jamie. He shuffled his feet. "I wanted to." I stared at him. There was a word for what I was feeling in that moment—I just couldn't name it.

We went upstairs and I stood in front of the mirror as Jamie clasped the chain around my neck. Then he slipped his hands around my waist from behind. My eyes fluttered closed. His lips found my neck. I turned around and began to take off his clothes. We collapsed onto my bed. Jamie's hand slid down my stomach.

"How is vanilla your favourite ice cream flavour?"

I groaned and shut the cutlery drawer with a rattle. Jamie sat with his elbows on the kitchen counter, his eyes following me with an amused glint. A tub of vanilla ice cream sat between us.

"It's always the same," I said.

"So is chocolate."

"No way. Chocolate is always different."

Jamie continued to smirk at me. I glared at him and he burst out laughing. "So even five-year-old Joni thought that vanilla was a better flavour than chocolate or strawberry?" Jamie demanded.

I opened the ice cream lid but it was still too frozen to eat. "Well, it used to be the rainbow flavour—you know the one sold at the parlour at the mall?"

Jamie nodded. "Tastes like bubblegum."

"Yeah. But as a kid the blue food colouring made me hyper so my parents started ordering vanilla for me instead." I shrugged. "Somehow it just stuck."

"I'm buying you rainbow ice cream tomorrow," he said with a laugh. "We'll see if it still has the same effect."

"Very funny." I dug my spoon into the ice cream and managed to scoop some out, the metal bending slightly under the pressure.

"How's your sister?" Jamie asked.

I stared down at my spoon, my distorted reflection visible in the metal. "I haven't heard from her." It was the truth. I hadn't heard from Ellie since she called to tell me her flight had landed safely. She texted photos occasionally so I knew she was alive, but she hadn't called.

"She's not just away for the summer," said Jamie. I shook my head. Jamie stared down at the tub of ice cream. He took a deep breath in, as if readying himself to say something but at the last moment he let it out in a sigh. He turned his spoon around in his fingers. He said, "Maybe vanilla isn't so bad after all."

We sat down on the sofa after the ice cream and put on the second *Impossible Identity* movie. The dramatic theme music started up and I settled back into Jamie's arms. The opening scene flickered to life and we began to poke fun at the unrealistic action sequences and how the lead actor's hair remained perfect despite epic fight scenes and scaling multi-storey buildings.

"I like being here," Jamie said suddenly. I didn't know how to respond, so I kissed the back of his hand and settled against him.

I wanted to say, *I like being here, too.*

I didn't know what to do with myself when I couldn't see Jamie. We spent nearly every day together so it was strange when he couldn't come over. I forgot that he had a family that cared about where he was.

I hadn't seen Mum in weeks. I think she came home one morning before work to pick up more of her clothes. She was permanently with Jacky, drinking herself out of a liver. At this point I thought it was more likely that I'd see Dad again.

I decided to drive to the mall as I wanted a new bikini and that's what I'd done before Jamie anyway. Mum and Dad had set up an allowance for me, meaning I got money once a month and seeing as I usually stayed at home not doing anything, I had a lot to spend. It was soothing, spending money and watching my bags fill up. It gave me purpose.

I went to the surf store and bought the two bikinis I really wanted. I also picked up a new beach towel and an inflatable donut ring for the pool. I could imagine Jamie lounging on it in the sun, his eyes shut as the sun kissed the panes of his chest. The thought made me smile and I checked my phone in case he'd called. He hadn't.

I went to the bookstore and found a copy of *Persuasion* by Jane Austen. Ellie had been begging me to read it for years and the thought of doing it now made me feel closer to her. I purchased the book and was trying to fit my credit card back into my purse when I ran straight into Skye Matthews. Etta's best friend. Her shopping bags fell to the ground with a thud.

"Oh my god!" I exclaimed and reached to pick up her bags, but she beat me to it. I straightened up and she glared at me. "I'm really sorry," I said. "I hope there wasn't anything breakable in there." I was going to offer some money to cover anything broken but something in the way Skye's lip curled stopped me.

"I'm not the one you should be apologising to," Skye clipped.

I blinked. "I don't know—"

"How does it feel to have someone's leftovers?"

"What?" My throat closed up and I couldn't say anything else.

"You think that he likes you, but you're

wrong," Skye continued and my body froze. "You're his rebound—an afterthought. She was with him first."

"I don't know what you're talking about," I managed to whisper. My eyes stung and I knew if I blinked then tears would start to fall.

Skye laughed and the sound pierced through me. Her eyes turned to stone. "Everyone knows. You don't have to put on an act. Everyone knows you're fucking Jamie Akerman."

I flinched at his name. I wanted to say something. I wanted to cry and tell her to mind her own business, but I couldn't make my mouth move. "Whatever," said Skye. "Enjoy him while he lasts." Then she turned and walked away.

I stood frozen in shock until a group of thirteen year olds pushed past me and I realised I was blocking the entrance to the shop. I went straight to the carpark. It might have been better for me to keep shopping and distract myself but I didn't want to risk running into Skye again. What if Etta was there too?

I sat in my car and locked the doors. I felt dirty, guilt dripping over me like sweat. I didn't turn on the engine. I sat with my useless purchases in the back and buried my head on the steering wheel. The dance flashed before my eyes—Etta's face looking down at me and Jamie like a wounded animal who had been shot in the chest by her owner. How, after all this time spent with Jamie, had I forgotten about the dance and the other girl he had gone to the dance with? I let myself cry. I heaved until there was nothing left in me to come out.

At home I unpacked my purchases on the kitchen counter, trying to decide which bikini to wear. A sudden muffled sound coming from my bag told me that my phone was ringing. It was Jamie. There were already two messages from him asking if I was home. I hadn't heard them even though my phone wasn't on silent. I quickly answered his call before it went to voicemail.

"Hey."

"Hey," came Jamie's reply, his voice scratchy down the line. "How was your day?"

"I went to the mall," I said.

"Cool. Did you buy anything?"

"Bathers. A book."

"Sounds nice." A beat. "I missed you today," he said.

I swallowed. There was a lump in my throat. "Okay."

To my surprise, he laughed. My cheeks burned and I was grateful that he couldn't see me.

"I mean it," Jamie said. I nodded but didn't say anything. His tone changed. "Joni, are you okay?"

"Yeah," I said too brightly. "Fine. Perfectly fine."

"If you're not fine I can come and see you. I've finished all the errands Nora enslaved me to do today."

I wanted to see him but I didn't want him to see me like this. "No, please," I said. "I'm okay—just tired from the mall. I'll see you tomorrow?"

"Yeah," Jamie said after a pause, his voice slightly uneven. "I'll see you tomorrow then."

"Jamie?"

"Yeah, Joni?"

"I missed you, too."

I could hear him smiling down the line. "See you tomorrow," he said, and we hung up.

I still wanted to know what happened to the missing photo of me and Ellie. It had been bothering me ever since I noticed it was gone. I was so paranoid about it that I almost called Mum and demanded she come home to tell me where it was. I couldn't explain why, but it was important to me.

I'd searched the entire house for it and even

made Jamie look with me as a second pair of eyes. "What is it about this photo?" he'd joked at one stage. Then I told him that we weren't having sex until we found it and he continued searching with twice the attentiveness.

It was ridiculous to care so much. But it kept me distracted from what happened at the mall with Skye. *Enjoy him while he lasts.* I felt sick every time I thought about her words. *Would* Jamie leave me? I didn't think I would survive if he did.

I spent the day with Jamie searching the house to no avail before he pulled me into his arms and then onto the sofa. I laughed as he tickled my belly—when had he discovered that I was ticklish?—and begged him to stop. We both tried to catch our breath—tangled together, his head above mine.

"Do you miss him?" Jamie asked. I knew who he meant.

"He left in the night. No goodbye. No note. Not even a voicemail. The day after Christmas."

"I'm sorry."

"Worse things have happened to people," I said.

"Doesn't make it easier. School must have been difficult after that," said Jamie after a moment. "You weren't…yourself."

"I didn't have anyone to talk to," I said into his

shoulder.

Jamie nodded. "No one deserves that." He stroked my hair back and I closed my eyes. "We'll find the photo," he said and I nodded. "We might have to break your no sex rule though," he added. I choked out a laugh. He held me close and kissed me softly and kept me next to his heartbeat until nightfall.

"I'm not staying," Mum greeted me the next day. She found me in the kitchen eating a bacon sandwich and crisps. I hadn't heard her come in, having been in the middle of composing a perfect response to Jamie's latest message. He was coming over later and we were arguing over what to watch now that we'd finished the *Impossible Identity* series.

I nearly stood up in shock. "Hi," I said, through a mouthful of crisps.

"I'm just here to put on some laundry and take some new clothes back to Jacky's." She didn't even look in my direction as she hauled an overnight bag I assumed was full of clothes into the laundry room. I abandoned my food and followed her.

I stood in the threshold with my arms folded, watching as she unloaded her bag and dumped clothes into the machine. I couldn't remember the last time I'd seen her. I couldn't remember the last time I'd seen her sober.

I tucked my hair behind my ears. "How are you?"

"Jacky's a real angel," Mum said. She reached for the laundry powder. "She was a smart woman for never getting married. Take note, Joni." I said nothing and she turned on the machine. It started up with a beep and she shut the door so hard I flinched.

"How's work?" I tried again.

"It's work. I go, they treat me like shit and then I get paid at the end of the month." I decided not to argue with that. Mum pushed past me. "Your sister called. She's extending her trip."

"Ellie called?" A stab of hurt pulsed through me. "Is she okay?" I followed her upstairs and into her bedroom. I'd cleaned the room while she was gone, opening the windows and the curtains and clearing the vodka bottles from under the bed.

"She's fine, Joni," Mum snapped. "Concern yourself with your own life."

I sat on the edge of the bed as Mum disappeared into the wardrobe. "I just hadn't heard from her. I assumed she'd stay in touch a bit more." My heart ached at the mention of Ellie and how she'd called Mum and not me. Mum reappeared carrying an armful of clothes. She stuck them on the bed next to me and gestured for me to help her fold them. I took a deep breath. "How long are you staying at Jacky's for?"

"I don't know."

"Will you be back before school starts? It's my final year—they have parent nights in September."

"I'll figure it out," Mum said in a tone I'd heard from her too many times before. Her word was final.

I tugged on the loose threads of a blouse I was meant to be folding. "I'm seeing someone." I don't know why I told her. I don't know what I wanted from it. I don't know what I expected.

Her face became rigid. She stopped folding and looked up at me, her expression frosty. "Well don't come crying to me when they leave you." I felt the air rush out of my lungs. My throat swelled up and I couldn't speak. She looked me up and down. "I can't think of any reason why they would want to stay."

My hands shook. I put the blouse down and went back to the kitchen. I finished my sandwich. She came back down ten minutes later, her bag full of new clothes. "Hang my washing up when it's done," she called, not stopping to talk. The front door slammed behind her.

***

Something was wrong with Jamie. He arrived at mine later than I expected and without the usual buoyancy in his step. We had sex and then laid on top of my bedcovers, our naked bodies sprawled together.

My phone kept flashing and vibrating on the bedside table beside me. "You're popular this morning," Jamie observed. He nodded towards it. "Do you want to answer whoever it is?"

"The volleyball group are having a party tonight," I explained and picked up the phone after another message from Lyn in the group chat. "Sort of an end of summer thing." It would be a typical affair. Empty house, paper cups, too much vodka and someone ending up with someone they shouldn't be with on Lyn's living room sofa. The next sentence fell out of my mouth before I could stop it. "You can come if you want—I mean I'm sure you're already invited."

"Do you even like those girls?" he asked.

"Sometimes," I said. I didn't really like Lyn, but some of the others were okay. "Why?"

"There was just this one time when you were playing volleyball…I don't know," he shrugged. "I just got the impression that they weren't really your friends."

"I haven't seen them since school. Might be good to go but I don't know…"

"We can go," he said. I must have given him a look because he nudged me and said, "We can go together if you like." His words made me smile but there was a distance in his voice. His eyes wouldn't meet mine completely.

Jamie wanted food and I wanted burgers, so I dressed and went into the garage where we kept the chest freezer. I pulled out the frozen patties as well as some rolls. Inside the house, Jamie turned the oven on and found cheese and tomatoes in the fridge. While the buns defrosted and the patties cooked, we sat on the sofa and watched TV. We'd started a sitcom from the nineties. I kept forgetting the name of it, but the women wore brown lipstick and the men had floppy haircuts.

Then the oven beeped and Jamie raced over to the kitchen. I laughed at him and told him to be patient before greeting a wall of heat as I opened the oven. Jamie liked his burger with everything on it, piled up so much that he almost couldn't eat it. I kept mine fairly plain, but added mayo, mustard and ketchup to which Jamie wrinkled his nose at.

We ate on the stools, the TV playing in the

background. I told him I wanted to swim afterwards. He said we should wait for our food to digest first.

Halfway through our burgers Jamie said suddenly, "Maybe we should drive to the beach before summer ends? Seeing as you love it so much. Then you can swim there too."

"That would be nice," I said and smiled into my burger. "We could stay in the beach house," I said as an afterthought. I hadn't seen my grandma in a few years and longed to be with her. My cheeks warmed at the thought of introducing her to Jamie.

"Is that where you take all your boyfriends?" he asked. His mouth always quirked to the left when he made a joke. It didn't move now.

"I don't have any ex-boyfriends," I said, shaking my head at him. "You know that."

"Neither do I," he said. "Nor ex-girlfriends for that matter."

The words were out of my mouth before I could think. "What about Etta?"

His body tensed. All lightness gone. He put down his burger but didn't look at me. "What *about* Etta?"

"I just—" I tripped over my words, his demeanour changed completely. I didn't want to upset him—the fragile butterfly with his already heavy wings. "I just thought you were…because of the dance," I stumbled. "I'm sorry."

"I haven't been friends with Etta since the night of the dance," Jamie said coldly. "She was never my girlfriend." He wiped his mouth with the back of his hand and stood up. I didn't believe him. His tone was too sharp, too short.

"Where are you going?" I asked, hoping it didn't sound like I was pleading with him.

"I forgot I have to run an errand for my mum," he said. I knew it was a lie. He grabbed his rucksack and then, almost as an afterthought, leant over and kissed my forehead. "I think it might run late so I can't come with you tonight. You have fun, though. I'll see you later."

I didn't go to the party. Instead, I texted my friends and told them I had a stomach bug and didn't want them to catch it. None of them responded; they were used to me bailing.

I put the TV on and sat not watching it, drinking cordial and eating a bowl of cherries instead of dinner. I kept checking my phone, waiting for Jamie's name to pop up. I turned my phone volume as loud as it would go but continued to look at it anyway. I drifted into a light and restless sleep where my face morphed into Etta's before my eyes shot open suddenly from the intro music for the Channel 2 News.

It was so hot in the living room that I opened all the windows and then the patio door. I wandered outside trying to breathe. The swimming pool glistened, reflecting the twilight sky. I unbuttoned my shorts, then pulled my t-shirt over my head. I jumped into the pool with a loud splash.

The water greeted me with open arms and I let myself be taken. I swam laps until the cold seeped deep into my bones. Being underwater cleared my head, the rushing in my ears drowning out my worries—even for only a moment.

Afterwards, I showered and changed into my favourite striped pyjamas and went back downstairs. Then I checked the locks before collapsing onto the sofa. I looked at my phone. There was still no message or call from Jamie.

It dawned on me that Jamie might be my only friend. My friends at school liked volleyball Joni. Joni who played well at competitions and went out for pizza afterwards and smiled at them and rolled her eyes when they told her she was the silent killer of the group. They loved that Joni, but they didn't love this one—the empty shell who didn't know how to occupy herself on a Friday night.

I called Ellie. She answered straight away. "Joni?"

"Ellie!" I exclaimed, thrown off by her promptness. "I thought I'd see if I could catch you." I paused. "What time is it there?"

"Early," she said. There was noise in the background, street sounds and cars and music. People yelling. I had no idea where she was. "I went out dancing again," she said. "You didn't wake me."

"That sounds like fun," I said.

"What have you been up to?"

"I went swimming tonight."

"Alone?"

"This time."

That piqued Ellie's interest. "Well that doesn't sound boring," she said. "Who have you not been swimming with?"

"No one you'd know," I said, and Ellie snorted.

"Everyone knows everyone in Cedar," she said. Before this summer I might have laughed and agreed with her. I was beginning to realise that people in Cedar thought they knew everything about everyone but perhaps the truth lay under the surface. There was a whole other side to everyone that none of us knew—the real Cedar.

"Did you take that photo from the living room with you?" I said abruptly.

"Huh?" There was a sudden surge in the voices around her.

I raised my voice. "You know, the photo of us on our bikes in Grandma's garden."

"I haven't taken any photos—look can I call you later? We need to catch this train. Bye!"

The line crackled then went flat. I stared at the phone. I should have asked her about the photo from the beginning. I should have asked her where she was. Maybe she didn't want me to know—she was truly free.

I flicked through the TV channels until I settled for a movie set in Notting Hill I'd seen a dozen times before. Jamie didn't call—I suppose he thought that I'd actually gone to the party—and I ended up falling asleep on the sofa with the TV still on.

Jamie surprised me the next morning by driving to my house. He usually went everywhere on his bike, so I hadn't considered that he could drive or had a car to drive. I watched from the window as he pulled up and was out of the house before he even parked.

He rolled down the window, eyes trailing over my damp hair from the shower. "I thought I would drive you somewhere," he said from the car. "Just for a change." His face was paler than usual, eyes red.

"Let me get my shoes," I told him and ran back in the house.

When I got in the car he unbuckled his seatbelt and pulled me into him. I let out a small sound of surprise before he released me.

"I'm sorry I snapped at you yesterday," he said.

"It's okay," I replied, still unsure and assessing him carefully.

Jamie gripped the steering wheel and drove down my road and away from school and the centre of town. We drove up the winding roads to the very edge of Cedar where there was a lookout. The manicured trees in the suburbs gave way to verges of tall pine trees on either side of the road. Lush greenery, shrubs, pink lilies and yellow daisies grew at the bottom of trees. Brown birds with periwinkle chests nested in branches, swooping down and flying past the window. Cedar was beautiful without the people.

The lookout was empty. There were rumours it was haunted. I supposed that really kept everyone away. Jamie turned the engine off and cracked open his window. The weather was cooler today, a gentle breeze and overcast sky.

He took a deep breath. "I think we should talk about the dance."

My heart immediately began beating in double time. "We don't have to," I said. "I'm sorry I made it weird yesterday." I didn't want to be here. I wanted it to be yesterday when we were on the sofa. I wanted to take back what I'd said.

"I don't want you to be sorry. I want to explain."

"Okay," I said in a quiet voice.

"I shouldn't have kissed you that night."

"I know."

"I went to the dance with…but when I found you—"

"It's okay." How many times was I going to say that? "I understand." He was leaving me and all I could think was that Mum had been right.

Jamie frowned, then ran his hands through his hair. "I'm fucking this up so bad," he said. His attention turned to something on the backseat of the car and for the briefest moment I saw a flicker of panic across his face. I turned in my seat.

It was a cream cardigan with an embroidered sunflower on the left breast. It was so familiar and

I should have known straight away but it took me a moment to place it, to understand who it belonged to.

My eyes stung and the little colour in Jamie's face drained. "Joni," he managed to say. "It's not what you think."

I felt like I'd left my body and I was hovering over us, watching the scene unfold from above. Had he been seeing her this entire time? When he looked at me, did he see her?

Bright blonde hair; emerald dress; wildflowers. *What the fuck?*

Jamie didn't know me at all. All those stories I had told him. All the colours I had given. He hadn't seen me through any of it. It had always been *her*. I remembered our first kiss but now I couldn't remember our last.

This was karma, wasn't it? I'd done wrong the night of the dance. We'd kissed in the classroom while he'd been with someone else. He was never mine to keep in the first place.

I was out of the car in one sweeping movement. August was over. I felt it plummet away from me in that instance. Jamie was over.

"No! Joni. Please."

I slammed the door and didn't look back, knowing that if I did he wouldn't be asking me to stay. Jamie would be clinging to the cardigan, watching me leave.

ETTA

I first spoke to him in the grocery line. He was
wearing his school uniform and arguing with a
woman I assumed was his mum. They looked
identical, almost. Big expressive eyes and dark, curly
hair. I sat behind him in Biology, his head always
bobbing up and down as he watched the whiteboard
and copied the notes. I felt like we were meant to
meet each other. It was a fanciful feeling based off no
reason—but I couldn't shake it.

I waved off Jacky Carson and "Silent Night"
started playing for the thirteenth time that afternoon. I
adjusted the tin of candy canes on the counter; though

I'd refused to wear the reindeer ears that had been left out for me. I was grateful for that choice as Jamie Akerman appeared before me.

His mum gave me a big smile that showed all her teeth. "How are you today?"

"Same old," I said. I noticed they were buying potatoes and two chickens—which were currently on special—and a mix of fresh and tinned vegetables. "Are you doing a roast tonight?"

"Yes," she said with an even bigger smile. "We're celebrating Christmas this weekend because my husband will be out of town during the actual Christmas break, although Jamie thinks it's ridiculous." She pointed at the two of us. "I assume you two must know each other from school?" She began digging in her bag for her wallet.

"I'm in the year below. But we have Biology together." I glanced at Jamie, but looking at him made my ears turn pink.

"You sit behind me," he said, his eyes meeting mine. I wanted to paint them. I wondered how many colours I would need to mix to get that exact shade of brown.

"Yeah, I don't really have any friends in the class," I said, regretting each word as it came out of my mouth. I went back to focusing on the till, willing my cheeks to cool down.

"But do you like the class?" Jamie asked.

"Not really," I said without thinking. A smile started to grow on his mouth. "I just mean that I've had better teachers. I expected more practicals." I packed a bag of salt and vinegar crisps and looked up at him.

"I agree," Jamie said. We stared at each other and neither of us looked away.

The card machine pinged in the background as Jamie's mum paid. "Help me with the bags, please," she said and passed some over to him. The receipt printed from the machine.

"Nice cardigan," Jamie said.

"Thanks." My voice matched his. We were staring at each other openly now.

"Well, that was delightful," Jamie's mum cut in. "It was nice speaking with you, Etta. Have a lovely Christmas if we don't see you before then."

I broke the spell between us and turned to her. "Happy Christmas, Mrs Akerman."

"See you in class," said Jamie, and he waved goodbye.

"Perhaps," I replied, and began scanning in the next customer's groceries.

***

The big news in town dropped after Christmas. Dad came home from the gym and told me. He had a gym membership but only ever used the swimming pool. There was something endearing about how he continued to swim throughout winter—leaving the house when it was still dark, wrapped up in his coat with his sports bag, and coming home with damp hair and smelling of chlorine.

"Leonard Fraser has left town," Dad greeted me with. He came in the back door, placing his bag in the usual spot underneath the coats.

I was in the middle of making a cup of tea before school. "No!" I gasped, nearly knocking the mug off the counter. "But I just saw him before Christmas."

"Yes!" Dad mimicked in the same shocked tone. "And watch what you're doing."

"Why?" I asked, using a teaspoon to push the teabag around the mug. The toffee-coloured water deepened.

"Because I don't want to have to clean up after you," Dad said drily. I rolled my eyes and motioned for him to go on. "He's been unhappy for years," Dad continued, taking a seat at the round kitchen table. "Leonard and Susannah got married after high school. It stopped Leonard taking his volleyball scholarship. Then she had the baby."

"Joni?"

Dad frowned, it deepened the already prevalent lines on his forehead. "No. Elena. She's the older one I think."

"How did you find out?" I asked.

"I overheard Jacky talking about it at the reception. Not very nicely either." Dad shuddered. I nodded. Jacky Carson was the worst Cedar had to offer. "Apparently Susannah isn't coping…" He trailed off and something about the silence that followed stopped me pressing for further details.

I took the tea bag out of my mug with the tips of my fingers, rushing to the bin before the hot water scolded me. I ignored Dad's cringe. "Well I'm sure that's all anyone is going to be talking about today." It was the first day back after Christmas break. I had Biology in the morning and I was already excited about the prospect of seeing the back of Jamie Akerman's head.

Dad shook his head and opened his morning paper with a flourish. "That's Cedar Valley for you. I'm surprised it hasn't made the morning news." At that moment, the backdoor swung open and

Skye came bundling through with a rush of cold air. "Morning, Skye," Dad said with a wave, not taking his eyes off the paper.

"Morning," Skye exhaled. She caught my eye and the familiar wild look split across her face.

"I already know about the Frasers," I said quickly.

Skye dropped her school bag to the floor and sank into the empty kitchen chair. "How?" she asked, looking deflated. I pointed at Dad. Skye raised her eyebrows and gave him an appraising look. "Not bad." Dad grunted and turned over his newspaper.

"Don't be a gossip," I warned. Skye poked her tongue out at me.

"Go to school," said Dad. He was right, we were going to be late. I drank as much of my tea as I could and ran out the door with Skye.

I didn't speak to Jamie the entire first week back. Or the second. I avoided him in Biology, so excited and nervous about him maybe turning around and talking to me that I moved seats. Or perhaps I was more afraid that he wouldn't acknowledge me—that our conversation in the grocery line meant nothing to him and I was an idiot for letting it play in my head like a film reel each night before I fell asleep.

The week passed in a blur of classes and school books. Friday arrived, and I sat on the tiny brick wall outside the assembly hall and opposite the bus station waiting for Skye to finish advanced maths. The bell rang and everyone started piling out of classrooms. There was the usual Friday afternoon lightness in the air. It didn't take long for Skye to make her way across the lawn to me, her frizzy hair pushed back with a lime green headband that was definitely not in line with the school uniform policy.

"I have news," she greeted me with once I was in earshot.

I smiled. "When do you not?"

Skye sat down then said seriously, but with the little flash of mischief in her eyes, "Joni Fraser spent all of lunch in the English classroom crying."

"How do you know that?" I asked. Skye had a way of overhearing everything and then relaying it all back to me. She was a gossip for sure but not like the others in Cedar. She didn't use the information to hurt people.

"I heard some of Joni's volleyball friends talking about it in the A-Block bathroom when I had my break in maths."

My stomach churned. "That's awful," I said. "If

it's true."

Skye shook her head. "Why wouldn't it be true?"

Joni was part of the volleyball team which meant that she was friends with the volleyball girls. They weren't the nicest lot going. I shrugged. "I hope she's okay."

"She's rich," said Skye. "She'll buy a new handbag or a car or a beach house and everything will be fine." Before I could reply Skye suddenly lowered her voice and leant towards me.

"Look who it is," she said under her breath, and tilted her head towards the doors to the assembly hall. I looked and then immediately looked away, my cheeks flaring. Skye rolled her eyes. "I don't know what you see in him." She squinted at him. "I suppose he's okay from a distance." When I didn't answer, she added, "Just call him over here—get to know him properly. You can't be in love with him after one conversation and a million hours spent staring at his head."

"I'm not in love with him," I managed to say through buttoned lips. I peeked another glance.

Jamie Akerman was strolling across the lawn with a group of friends. I'd noticed that Jamie didn't have a best friend in the way that I had Skye. He had lots of friends, always floating in the middle of groups. But even though he was never alone I couldn't help but look at him and think he was lonely.

Jamie's gaze suddenly caught on mine, like he could hear me thinking about him. He grinned.

"Shit."

"What?" questioned Skye.

"Pretend we're in the middle of a conversation," I insisted.

"Are you serious?"

I gulped. "I think he might be coming over here."

Skye's eyes widened. "He what?"

"We made eye contact."

"And that means he's coming over here?"

I grimaced. "No, I think he's coming over here because he *is*." I braved taking my eyes off Skye to watch as Jamie clapped his friends on the back and began walking in our direction.

"Holy shit," said Skye. She too was now looking, or glaring, rather. I hoped that Jamie didn't notice. He was fast approaching us and, my god, did he look really good.

"Hey," I called out once he was in earshot.

"Jeanette Anderson," Jamie greeted me evenly, using my goddamn full name. I blushed.

"Oh for the love of…" Skye muttered under her breath.

Jamie sat down behind Skye, causing her to shift her body so she wasn't blocking him out. She did it, but with a huff. "You moved in Biology," he said to me.

"Yeah, I moved because there was this huge head in my way and I couldn't see the board," I joked.

"I'll take that," said Jamie. I could have sworn he was trying to hide a smile. He gestured to both of us. "What are you two up to tonight?"

"We're going to an art gallery," said Skye pointedly.

"There's no art gallery in Cedar," Jamie frowned.

"We're taking the train to Willow Park," I said. "There's a great one there and it has this amazing cafe."

"Etta's an artist you know," Skye interrupted.

"I paint," I clarified. "Oils."

"That's very impressive," Jamie said, and he sounded genuine. "Why are you doing advanced biology then and not art?" he asked.

"Stupidity?" I said. He laughed and something inside of me warmed.

"You think she can't be an artist and a scientist?" Skye said pointedly. I had to roll my eyes at that. Skye could be so protective.

"I'm sure Etta can be whatever she wants," said Jamie.

Skye checked the silver watch clasped around her wrist that I had given her for her birthday last year. She poked my shoulder. "We'd better go if we're going to make the train." The train station was a five-minute walk from school. Skye looked directly at Jamie. "You coming with us or what, Akerman?"

Jamie had to buy a ticket at the station. I went every week with Skye so we had yearly passes. I liked our traditions.

I was thrilled to have Jamie with us and couldn't believe that he was coming—or that Skye had invited him. Skye caught me pinching myself on the train when Jamie wasn't looking and mimicked vomiting.

Willow Park Gallery was set at the top of a green hill, overlooking the town. In the warmer months, we sat outside on the grass with our school shirt sleeves rolled up.

We took Jamie to our favourite rooms in the gallery. I liked the bold, sometimes grotesque oil paintings, while Skye liked the abstract, brightly coloured works that resembled Matisse. I noticed that Jamie was a great listener. He took in whatever either of us said about the art, drinking it in with a curious smile and childlike eyes.

He liked one painting in particular. Skye had broken off from us, waggling her eyebrows as she told me she'd meet us in the cafe. I was petrified to be alone with him but also excited that we could talk in private. I stood with him by an impressionist piece of a sailboat and a seaside town in the background.

"This is nice," he said and for a moment I thought he meant us being there.

"I have another one you'll like," I said a little too fast. I took Jamie into the next room to stand in front of my favourite piece in the gallery: *Among Friends*. It was by a French artist, Monique Bardot. Her brush strokes were smooth and lucid. It turned the painting into a dreamy landscape of peaked cliffs, pale blue seas and a dense forest. Hues of violet trailed into the forest and navy speckled the bottom of the cliffs. It was one of those paintings I felt like I could step into and get lost in. Every time I saw it I discovered something new.

"I get why you come here every week," Jamie said. I blinked, disorientated. *How could he know?* Then I realised he meant the painting. Jamie liked the painting I had shown him. For the first time that day I let myself truly look at him. I took in the length of his neck, the way the ends of his hair curled at the nape of his neck, the hands he usually let swing by his sides.

"It's calming," he said, and nodded at the painting.

"It reminds you that there is a world outside of Cedar," I said. "Have you spotted the hidden figure in the painting?" I took a step closer, feeling the warmth radiating off his body.

"Hidden what?"

"Look." I gestured to the forest on the left of the canvas. Jamie fixed his gaze on where I had pointed. I took a deep breath. "It's nice that you're here."

"Why wouldn't I be?"

"Because you didn't know my name until your mum said it."

He paused then said, "Everyone knows everyone in Cedar."

I smiled, trying to hide my disappointment that he didn't seem to want to discuss it further. "I think that everyone believes they know everyone in Cedar from a glance," I said. "If we actually stopped to look closer then maybe we'd notice that there are many things not always on the surface."

"I see it!' Jamie suddenly cried out. His gaze fixed on the spot I had pointed out. It had taken him longer than I had thought but at least he'd gotten there.

"Knew you would," I said, and Jamie beamed at me. "We'd better go," I added. "Skye will be in a mood if they've run out of orange and poppy seed cake while she's waiting for us."

"More of a mood than usual?" Jamie teased. Then I surprised myself and reached out to shove him lightly. He laughed.

"She's protective!" I insisted.

"She doesn't like me," said Jamie.

"Give her a chance."

Jamie raised his hands in defeat. "Only if she gives me one."

At the cafe Skye was at our regular table by the window with three cappuccinos and three slices of orange and poppy seed cake. The sky was shifting from dark blue to indigo. It would be dark before we left.

Skye began quizzing Jamie on the different rooms and his favourite pieces. He answered each pf her questions with ease and by the end of her interrogation, Skye's lips quirked up. She was impressed.

"I think Jamie has shown great art enthusiast potential," Skye declared. "You are officially invited to Willow Park Fridays."

"I'd like that," Jamie said in a small voice. His gaze fixed on me.

All I could do was smile. We raised our coffee mugs and clicked them together. We got the last train home.

I had never had a real crush before. My crushes were daydreams I conjured in class. They were landscapes built from passing comments or bumping of arms as we walked together. Sometimes I had crushes on strangers I saw at the bus stop and I would create a personality for them and our entire life together.

My crush on Jamie was different. Jamie was flesh and conversation and reality. He joined us every week at Willow Park, wrapped up in his black overcoat and gloves as we trudged through the freezing air.

"You're in deep," Skye said one afternoon. I was at work and she was perched opposite me, her history textbook open on the counter. The store was dead and I had my own maths notes out, trying to convince myself that algebra would be useful in life.

I frowned. "What do you mean?"

"With Jamie."

"No I'm not," I said unconvincingly.

"It's okay," she said, flipping the page to a black and white photo of the Romanov family. "I actually like him."

I rolled my eyes. "Good to know."

"I think you two would be good together—" Skye stopped as the doors opened and Paige Stewart walked in. She returned my smile with a glare.

Skye lowered her voice. "And I think he likes you." I didn't know how to respond, my heart racing at the thought. "Maybe you should say something. I think things would go the way you want them to."

Her comments kept me up that night. I kept imagining Jamie at school and then at the gallery. He would follow me into one of the side rooms and stand so close to me I could feel the heat of his breath on my neck. Then he'd put his hand on the small of my back and turn me around and his brown eyes would slip down to my lips and—

I pulled my pillow over my head to block it all out.

The next day I went to the art department at lunch with Skye. Cedar Secondary cared about volleyball and little else. The gym was pristine with shiny courts and always smelt of new paint from where they were doing touch ups. The art department was a reflection of the rest of the school. The windows hadn't been cleaned in years, cobwebs forming on the outside across the panes and the wooden floor was covered in paint stains. Still, it was home for us; the one place we could be ourselves without the rest of the school's watchful glare.

Jamie joined us. I had been sure he'd still want to sit with his other friends at lunch but he seemed more than happy to be with us.

I was behind on my painting. I felt a block that had never been there before—a fear that if I went to the place I usually did when I created then I wouldn't be able to come back from it. I added to my canvas slowly and mixed colours as Jamie and Skye chatted away. They often got into heated debates with each other and I would stay quiet until I decided it was time to change the subject.

I was painting the mountains surrounding Cedar. Dad and I went camping there when I was a kid. We would canoe down the river and sit by a campfire in the evening. Our art project was to create something based around a significant person or place to you. I didn't like to plan my work. I preferred to start on a blank canvas and see where the paint took me. This time it dragged me to the mountains in autumn, where the air was crisp and the trees turned amber and gold.

Skye was explaining the project to Jamie as he looked over her photographs of the house she had grown up in that had sold recently.

"You should photograph Jamie for it," I joked.

"Very funny," Skye snapped.

"Have I not made an impact on your life?" Jamie prodded, mischief laced in his voice. "Am I not pretty enough for you?"

Skye started to smile. "Absolutely not," she said and I laughed. "Why don't *you* paint Jamie," Skye continued in a tone I didn't like. She looked directly at me and her words from the night before came swimming back. I focused my attention back to my canvas and said nothing. I didn't trust my voice to remain steady. "Fuck, I need to go. Can't be late to maths. I'm on my official last warning." I heard her laptop lid slam shut and the scraping of books on the table being swept into her bag. "I'll see you guys later," she called out and was gone.

I wasn't sure what to say to Jamie now that we were alone, so I kept working on my painting, mixing bright red and muted yellow together until it became burnt orange. I couldn't bring myself to look at him and I couldn't think of anything funny or interesting to say. Jamie remained quiet but I could feel his eyes on me. My cheeks grew warm.

I hadn't painted many portraits—it wasn't my strength—but the thought of painting Jamie was bewitching. I would capture him mid-laugh or the way his nose wrinkled when he wanted to disagree with Skye and knew he had to have a good argument to beat her. I longed to paint him standing at the *Among Friends* painting in Willow Park, shoulders square towards it, and eyes darting about it as he searched for the hidden meaning.

The bell rang and I began to clear up. Jamie waited for me at the table, staring out of the window. When I picked up my bag ready to leave he said, "I'll walk you to class."

I kept trying to start a conversation between us as we squished past people on the way to my locker, but every time I thought of something I couldn't get it out of my head. It was like the block I was having with my painting. I didn't know where it was coming from and I didn't know how to find my way around it.

"Is everything all right?" Jamie asked suddenly.

I snuck a look at him. "I'm just thinking," I said

and smiled to give him some reassurance. We reached my locker and I started throwing books in my bag.

"Thinking about what?"

Skye's voice resounded in my head, urging me to say something. I took a deep breath. "I like spending time with you." I barely got it out. For a moment I thought he hadn't heard me.

"Well, I like being friends with you, too," Jamie said. I waited for him to add something else. Anything else. He said nothing. That's not what Skye had assured me would happen.

I forced a smile. "Oh. Okay. I'll see you after school." My eyes began to sting and horror shot through me at the prospect of crying.

Jamie's brow furrowed. "I thought I was walking you to class."

"Can't have you being late!" I turned away before he could say anything else. I screwed my eyes closed as soon as my back was turned. A few hot tears leaked from the corners of my eyes. I wiped them with the back of my hand.

I told Skye what happened after school as we walked back to my house. "I think you're reading into it too much," she said after listening diligently. "It's not like you confessed your love for him."

I didn't believe her. I enjoyed being friends

with Jamie; he complemented me and Skye, added to what we already had rather than taking away from it. But I was frozen. I needed to hear something more from him, reassurance he couldn't or didn't want to give me.

"Etta? Etta are you listening to a word I'm saying?"

I shook my head, banishing certain thoughts from mind. Dad watched me from his checkered armchair, the pale glow of the TV reflected on his glasses. I gave him an apologetic smile. "Sorry, Dad. I don't know where my head went."

He spooned a mouthful of the green curry we'd ordered two hours earlier into his mouth. We were both slow eaters, dinners usually lasting hours because of it. Skye despaired with us whenever we invited her over to eat. She grew up with four brothers so had been bred to eat fast or not at all.

"What's going on? Is it something to do with school?" Dad asked.

I bit my lip. I was good at speaking to my dad about everything. In the weeks after Mum left, our shared grief was my only lifeline. He was the person who truly understood that loss and we had become closer because of it. However, this was about Jamie and I was still sixteen and apprehensive about talking to my dad about boys. I pulled the blanket on top of me to my chin, the fluffy material tickling against my skin. "It's Jamie," I said and, to my relief, Dad nodded in a knowing way.

"You don't have to say anything else," he assured me and I unclenched my jaw. "Boys are stupid. I would know, having been one myself. You have to spell it out to them. It's unfair, I know, but just tell him how you feel."

I couldn't tell Jamie how I felt. So I tried to show him. When I hugged Skye goodbye, I also hugged Jamie. I sat as close to him as I could in Biology, practically wishing the energy between us to spark into something.

Skye caught on to what I was doing, or at least attempting to. She started going to maths earlier and earlier and inventing reasons to leave us alone together. I had never really flirted before—I didn't know how in the way the volleyball girls did. I looked it up on my phone one night when I couldn't sleep but got too embarrassed to read any of the answers.

My tactics, however ridiculous they seemed to me, were working. Sort of. I was spending more time with Jamie and I no longer felt the anxiety I used to get when falling into conversations with him.

Although Jamie didn't like talking about himself, I learnt that his dad travelled for work and brought his mum back fridge magnets from every city. I knew his mum didn't work and a lot of women in Cedar judged her for that. Jamie didn't have a car but shared a family one with his two sisters, Nora and Samantha. He loved them both but said that Sam was easier to talk to. I also discovered, whether he wanted me to or not, that Jamie was a people pleaser. He was careful to never offend, even at the expense of not always saying what he meant.

We sat on the wall on a Friday late in March waiting for Skye to finish class, my uniform blazer draped over my lap. Jamie was going on about his family in a voice that was beginning to grate on me. Nora had pissed him off and he was going on about how he will probably end up moving out before either of his sisters and how he wished they do it sooner.

"You'd miss them," I snapped, interrupting his rant mid-sentence. "You would miss Sam, and even Nora if they moved out. The thing is that you never know what you have until it's gone." Jamie stared at me with a blank expression on his face. I clasped my hands together and avoided his gaze, worried I'd gone too far.

"I would," said Jamie finally in a quiet voice. "I would miss them. You're right—" He ran a hand through his hair and shook his head. "You're my best friend, Etta."

That proclamation changed something for me. A light switch turned on, an understanding—hope. I was his best friend, something no one else in his year had managed to be. I had a crush on Jamie Akerman and there really wasn't much to be done about it.

It was Saturday night and Jamie had agreed to come with us to Marigolds's party. Mari was in my art class and one of the few people I liked at school besides Skye and Jamie. Her parents were rich and often out of town, leaving Mari with a large empty house and pool for the weekend.

I liked going to her parties. I liked the ritual of dressing up and feeling the sparkly possibilities of the evening.

The house was as I remembered it with a long, paved driveway, bright red front door and three imposing stories towering above us. The driveway was lined with lights and they cast a bright glow against the enormous glass windows of the house.

Jamie arrived before us, sitting on the front

steps of the house. I caught him hiding a bottle of wine when he noticed us pull up. Though he didn't need to worry because it was Skye's oldest brother driving anyway.

When I got out of the car, I swear Jamie did a double take. I'd changed my outfit at least ten times before Skye had yelled at me to just wear the black dress I bought from the thrift store. It was sequinned with feathery tassels swishing at the hem. I wore dark red lipstick and shimmering silver eyeshadow. Dad had taken one look at me and said I looked like Daisy Buchanan.

"You drunk already, Jamie?" Skye called out, waving goodbye to her brother.

"I'm not sober," Jamie said meekly. He got to his feet with a small stumble.

Skye pressed her lips together, hiding a smile as she knocked on the door. "Should be an interesting night then."

It was the usual group at the party. Most of the art class and a few of Mari's other friends. Jamie was drinking his wine as if he expected it to be taken away from him at any moment. More than half the bottle was gone. He hadn't escaped the notice from some of the other girls.

"Your boy is gorgeous," Lena told me while I

waited behind her in line for the bathroom.

I blushed. "He's not my boy. He's just Jamie."

"That's not what everyone else is saying." She waggled her eyebrows. "Plus, he can't keep his eyes off you."

"He's drunk."

Lena shrugged. "Might make him more talkative."

I rejoined Jamie and the others in the upstairs lounge decorated with a thick, cream rug that tickled my feet. Jamie was throwing his arms everywhere as if making an important point. The bottle of wine nearly slipped from his hand.

"Oh no you don't," Skye remarked, and I reached out and took the wine from Jamie. He stuck his bottom lip out, which made the other girls coo.

Eventually the girls trailed out of the room as the upstairs kitchen became the dance floor, music and thuds emanating from the ceiling. Skye winked at me as she left the room with Lena. I was alone with Jamie.

"All alone," Jamie sang.

"Yes," I said and took a swig of his wine.

Jamie's eyes met mine. "I want to see the stars."

I couldn't help but laugh. "You what?"

"The stars, Etta," he repeated with a sense of urgency. "We have to see the stars."

"All right. We'll go see the stars."

"You're very pretty," he added.

I paused and something unfurled inside of me. Every muscle in my body softened and I watched Jamie's big, brown eyes blinking at me as he waited for my response. "You're very pretty too," I said finally. He exhaled with a small smile.

The street was empty and the sky was too. Spring blossoms perfumed the air and there was a bite to the wind that made me wrap my arms around my body. Music and laughter echoed from the upstairs windows of the house.

Jamie stared up at the blank sky then shrugged. "The thing about stars," he sighed, "is that they are poems we cannot read." The wine slowed his words.

I opened my mouth and then frowned. "That makes no sense."

"Yeah," he nodded solemnly, "that's because I am drunk."

"That you are, Jamie."

His tone shifted. "Am I embarrassing?"

"You're hilarious."

"And you're very pretty."

There it was again, and although I knew he was

drunk I still craved the compliment. "Are you flirting with me?"

He gave a lazy smile. "Is it working?"

My heart stopped. I'd read in books, heard in music, listened to countless people, Skye included, talk about how your heart raced when you were with the someone you liked. But when I was with Jamie and he said things like that—it stopped.

"Maybe," I managed to say.

He closed his eyes. "Etta, how come you're not as drunk as me?"

"Because you had a bottle and a half and I had two glasses."

"Oh."

I inhaled sharply. It was now or never. "I love how you say my name."

"Come to the dance with me," he blurted out, eyes wide. I startled. He meant the end of year dance in June. I blushed. "Come on!" Jamie insisted. "It'll be fun."

"Okay," I laughed, unsure whether he would remember the invitation tomorrow morning when the drunkenness was replaced by a hangover. "I'll go to the dance with you."

Jamie's face split into a grin. "Thank you," he said. Then he pointed at the sky. "And that, everyone, is the poetry of the stars."

I heard the swing of the door and then Skye's voice called out, "Are you two coming back or what?" I knew that if I turned then she would have one eyebrow arched and her hands on her hips.

"Jamie needed air," I yelled.

"Actually I wanted to see the stars," Jamie slurred. Then he threw up.

Skye groaned and I heard the door slam shut. He'd narrowly missed my shoes. I shuffled away as he continued to retch, tentatively placing a hand on his shoulder until he finished. Skye returned with a glass of water and Jamie's phone.

"I texted his sister. Idiot doesn't even have a password on his phone." She rolled her eyes. Jamie started recover and Skye shoved the glass in his hand. "Small sips," she instructed.

Jamie was quiet while we waited for his sister to arrive. Eventually we heard the tires rolling on the driveway and we were bathed in white light. The car pulled up and Sam's head shot out of the window. "Are you going to throw up in my car?" she demanded over the hum of the engine.

"He should be fine," I said. I looked over at Jamie, who looked like he was going to pass out. Sam directed her attention to me. She had Jamie's eyes. "Just needs to go to bed," I finished with a smile. Sam shrugged and told Jamie to get in the car. Jamie pulled himself to his feet with a small wobble. Instinctively, I reached out and steadied his arm. He waved to Skye, who was hovering by the door.

"Enjoy your hangover!" she called to him.

"I had fun tonight," I said to Jamie.

"Me too," he agreed. He ran a hand at the nape of his neck. "Besides the whole throwing up. Sorry about that."

Without thinking, I went up on the tips of my toes, and kissed his right cheek. Jamie froze, but softened by the time I went back down. "Sleep well." Then, unable to look at him anymore, I walked up the steps to join Skye. Sam yelled at Jamie again and he opened the passenger door and got in. The car sped away until the place was quiet again.

"I told you he likes you," Skye said. I laughed and gave her a side hug. "Want to go inside?"

"In a minute," I said, feeling dazed and giddy. "I want to sit outside for a bit longer—take in the poetry of stars."

Jamie returned the next morning with bleary eyes and damp hair. I saw him while sitting on the front porch with my morning coffee in hand. Dad had been outside with me, reading the paper before he disappeared for a shower. Sunday mornings were our time to catch up with each other before another week began.

Jamie stopped in front of the house and rolled down the window. I waved.

"Get in the car," he said. I raised my eyebrows and he quickly added, "Only if you want of course."

"I'm in my pyjamas," I said.

"You're in the same cardigan you always wear. Besides, you don't need to be dressed up for this. You won't even have to leave the car."

I considered, though I already knew what I was going to do. "Let me put my mug inside and tell Dad," I said and ran inside.

I brushed my teeth and ran a brush through my hair and then rinsed out my mug. By the time I was done, Dad was out of the shower and making himself some toast.

"Is it okay if I go for a drive with Jamie?" I asked.

"Do I ever get to meet this Jamie?" Dad asked.

"You can meet him now if you like."

"And risk my toast going cold and soggy or black and burnt?" He scoffed. "I don't think so." He brought the butter and apricot jam out of the fridge. "Go," he said. "Have fun and don't get pregnant."

I gave him a quick hug. "Don't be gross, Dad."

Jamie was scrolling through his phone when I opened the door. When he saw me he shoved it back in his pocket. "You ready?" he asked, eyes bright.

I buckled my seatbelt and said, "As long as you're not taking me to the woods to kill me."

"Damn. Plan B it is then."

We pulled out of my street and made our way through the centre of Cedar. We were quiet on the drive. Jamie kept the windows down so the air rustled through us. The grocery store flashed by, next to it the pharmacy and the corner shop where they sold underage kids cigarettes if you paid them enough.

"How are you feeling after last night?" I tried to keep my voice as light as possible.

Jamie kept his eyes on the road. "Sorry about that."

"Don't be sorry," I said. "It was fun."

I stared out the window as the houses gave way to enormous pine trees and the wildflowers that grew at the base of them. In autumn, rings of toadstools dotted the ground and when I was a kid I believed that fairies lived inside them.

Jamie drove us to the edge of town. I knew

where we were going the moment he took the exit heading west.

The Cedar lookout was hardly used. There was a legend that it was haunted by a townswoman who went mad from trying to get revenge on her cheating ex-husband. She was said to have thrown herself off the ledge to try and win him back.

Jamie pulled into a spot and cut the engine. Cedar sprawled before us like Lego houses, a green patch where the park was. Jamie unbuckled his seatbelt and I did the same.

"I don't remember everything from last night," Jamie began slowly. "I mean I don't know if you know this but I was very drunk."

"Very funny." My voice caught in my throat. Jamie looked over to meet my gaze. In that look I knew everything.

He came here to kiss me.

"I like that cardigan," he said.

"It's pretty old. I should get a new one but I find it hard to let go."

"Then don't," he said.

It was a funny thing, the moment before a kiss. There was static, anticipation and the strong desire to laugh because it was absured that someone so wonderful was leaning towards you.

I thought that maybe in twenty years' time they'd tell the story about how we came here hungover and kissed in the car. Maybe they would but with wistful tongues and melancholy because they already knew the ending.

Jamie came towards me, his lips falling on mine.

We spent the weekends leading up to the dance at the lookout. I longed for every Saturday morning when Jamie would pick me up and drive us along the winding streets out of Cedar. Nothing changed between us at school or when we went to Willow Park with Skye. But at the lookout we were Etta and Jamie—Jamie and Etta. The dance was our first public event.

I woke up early on the day of the dance, just as the sun bled through my curtains. Dad had let me decorate my room last year and I'd indulged in bright yellows and dusky pinks and curtains with tiny flowers dotted across the fabric. I sat in the kitchen eating cinnamon sugar sprinkled on toast. Dad came home from the pool around noon and I decided to shower and get ready even though the dance wasn't until seven.

I laid out all my makeup on the dressing table. I lined my eyes with little flicks on the end like I'd seen in black and white movies. I powdered my face and smothered my lips in red lipstick. My hair took longer as I meticulously blow dried and curled it until it hung in sleek waves past my shoulders. When I was done I walked into the living room where Dad was watching TV. The sun had dipped in the sky enough that he had the lamps on. He clicked the remote when he saw me. "Wow," he exclaimed.

I gave a small twirl. I wore an emerald silk dress that hugged my body down to just above my ankles. My jewellery was a mixture of birthday presents from Skye and old pieces from my mum's jewellery box. She'd never taken anything with her when she left—as if nothing had been good enough for her.

Jamie arrived at my house on time wearing a midnight blue jacket, crisp white shirt and matching tie. His hair was freshly washed and he smelt of cedar wood and oranges.

He came in and shook hands with my dad who gave an approving nod to me when Jamie had his back to us. Then Jamie handed me a bunch of yellow sunflowers. "I guess you kind of know why," he said with a small smile. My heart grew three times its size.

We posed for photos on the front step, Jamie placing his hand on my waist. I could feel the warmth of his skin through the fabric of my dress. A shiver ran through me. Dad kept clicking away with the camera, trying to find new angles so we had candid ones, too: me and Jamie laughing at something, me trying to shove him away. I loved those photos. I loved being the girl in them too.

Afterwards, Dad packed us in the car and drove us to the school, dropping us out front with a wave and reminder to have fun.

A giant mirror ball hung from the ceiling of the gym. There were balloons in black and gold and vases of roses on tables with glass punch bowls. Confetti was everywhere and there was even a photo booth.

Someone had already spiked the punch when we arrived. Jamie confirmed this after taking one sip before pouring us small glasses. "We're not driving," he said, lifting his glass to clink it with mine.

"Etta!"

I whipped around. Skye practically ran across the gym to get to me, tottering in her too-high heels. She looked, if possible, even better than Jamie did. Her dress was startling silver and sparkled whenever she moved. Her dark skin glowed from the shimmer on her eyelids and her braided hair was styled into a bun on the top of her head. "You look hot," Skye exclaimed, her eyes running up and down me.

I swished my hips. "So do you."

"How's it going with Jamie?" Skye asked, her gaze darting over to him. He'd been alone when I left him but now Joe Scott was chatting with him.

"It's…" I took a deep breath. "It's wonderful."

Skye squeezed my hands. We drifted back over to Jamie once it looked like Joe wasn't going to leave him.

"You clean up well, Akerman." Skye teased, winking at him.

"Thanks," Jamie laughed. "You too." Then he looked at me. "Hey, so Joe wanted to know if we'd hang with him and some of my other friends?" Jamie nodded towards the tall blonde boy he'd been speaking to. I bit my lip. I felt paralysed suddenly.

"Hey, you must be Etta," Joe interrupted, stepping in and offering me his hand to shake. It seemed formal but something in the action relaxed me. He offered his hand to Skye too and I noticed her hold it a moment longer, her eyes not leaving him.

"Nice to meet you," I said.

"Jamie tells me you're an artist," said Joe. I raised my eyebrows. I didn't think Jamie spoke about me to anyone.

"I am. Well, I paint."

Joe went on to ask me what I painted and included Skye in the conversation. Before I knew it, we had made it to the bleachers where the rest of Jamie's friends sat. A sharp pain in my stomach began but suddenly Jamie's hand was laced in mine and he squeezed. I held my head high.

Being with Jamie was like being with a celebrity. All of his friends were nice, which was surprising. Even the volleyball girls complimented my outfit and asked me and Skye about our uni plans. Skye looked like she might pass out from shock. We sat with them until a piano cover of "Make You Feel My Love" came on. I looked up at Jamie and he laughed, reading the question on my face. He took my hand and we made it out onto the dance floor.

Jamie held me tightly as we swayed. He was warm and I felt safe with him. I hadn't felt safe in years. I nearly told him right there. I nearly told him about feeling safe with him and about my mum and about how I never wanted it to end between us—whatever was happening. I wanted us to always go to the art department at lunch and Willow Park on Fridays and the lookout on the weekend. Instead, I said, "I'm really glad you asked me here tonight."

Jamie smiled. "I'm really glad you said yes."

"I like you a lot." I paused. "You make me really happy." He pulled me closer and I put my head against his chest. I had the sensation that we would have time for all the things I wanted to say to him. I was happy to be in the moment.

When the song ended, we fell back on the bleacher steps. I went over to Skye because she was giving me a look that said, *Get your ass over here right now and tell me what you spoke about.* I couldn't tell her, though. A few of the volleyball girls and Jamie's friends had joined us and we started up a debate about whether Mr Webber was attractive or if he only was when you sat at the back of his class. Skye was very vocal about the topic as she had been arguing over it for years now.

I noticed that Jamie wasn't listening. Lyn Clark whispered something in his ear. He frowned then snapped at something she said. Lyn shrugged, flipping her hair and began talking to someone else on her volleyball squad.

Jamie came over and squeezed my shoulder. "I'm just going to use the bathroom. I'll be back." He kissed the top of my head. I felt like I was living a fever dream. Was I even allowed to feel this happy?

Skye raised her eyebrows when he left. The

rest of the group went off to dance, leaving us alone. Another song started playing which kept the group on the dance floor. Jamie still hadn't returned. Skye said she wanted to check her dress because there was a tag sticking into her back and she was going to the bathroom. I waited. For the first time that evening I was alone. She returned five minutes later and I knew from the look on her face that something was wrong.

"What's up?" I asked. When she sat down her legs wouldn't stop bouncing up and down. Her face was pressed together like she was trying very hard to keep something in. She never kept things from me unless she knew it would hurt me. It had to be something to do with Jamie. The punch in my belly gurgled. He had been missing for ages now.

"Jamie is with Joni," Skye said in a rush. I could tell by the way her eyes couldn't focus that she was keeping more from me. Her gaze travelled around the room.

"So what?" I said trying to play it cool, but my voice went very high pitched at the end. I didn't even know that Joni had come to the dance, she had been avoiding large crowds all year. "I like Joni. It's not like he doesn't have other friends."

Skye pursed her lips. It made her look like her mum. She hated it when I pointed that out.

"Just tell me," I exhaled.

"Jamie isn't just *with* Joni." Her mouth remained open but silence fell upon her. I smoothed down my dress, hands shaking a little. "Go and see for yourself. If it's really nothing then you'll see that."

"Where are they?" I asked after a moment.

"English classroom. Miss Stanley's."

I left the gym. I didn't want to find them. I wanted Skye to be wrong and for the classroom to be empty and for Jamie to have been in the gym this entire time and for Joni to not be at the dance at all. My heart thundered in my ears.

The hallways were eerily quiet. My shoes clapped and clicked on the linoleum flooring, echoing around. I got to the classroom, where I had spent many hours, and took a deep breath. I opened the door.

I wanted to go back to the gym and then back in time to the lookout with Jamie's hands in my hair and the ghosts of Cedar around us.

Jamie and Joni were kissing.

He had her face cupped in his hands and his lips pressed to her's and his eyes were closed. She had been crying because her cheeks were red and splotchy.

It was definitely not a case of *she kissed me.*

My stomach dropped and I stood in the threshold of the classroom until one or both of them sensed me there and drew apart.

Jamie stared at me. He looked dazed, like the world was coming back to him after he had been spinning. But he didn't say anything.

"What the fuck," I whispered. I backed out of the room and Jamie scrambled to his feet and called after me. Joni stared at the floor. I didn't look back.

I marched through the hallways and straight into the gym. Behind me, I heard the door open and footsteps pound through the hallway. I walked faster. My heartbeat raced. I wanted to cry but I couldn't feel the tears. *Shouldn't I be crying by now?*

Skye was by my side the moment I entered the gym. "Are you okay?" she asked, studying me. "Was I right?" I nodded but she seemed to already know. She put an arm around my back. "Do you want to leave?"

I shook my head. Then nodded. "I don't know." Nausea rose in my throat. "Jamie will be coming back and I can't—"

"We're going," Skye said firmly. We practically sprinted to the carpark, ignoring the eyes that followed us. The sticky June air hit me as I made it outside. I tried to gulp in as much of it as I could. Beside me, Skye had her phone pressed to her ear and I could tell she was getting her brother to come and pick us up.

"He'll be two minutes," Skye said and hung up the phone.

"Thanks," I managed.

The school doors flung open and Jamie came rushing out. He saw us straight away and beelined our direction. "Etta, I'm so sorry—please let me explain."

I flinched away from him.

"You need to fucking stay away," Skye warned him in a vicious voice, stepping between us.

Jamie didn't move. He looked at me. "She was upset. I shouldn't have done that. I'm so sorry. I didn't mean to."

Skye saw red. "Oh, it just happened, did it? Tell me, Jamie, have you been fucking Joni Fraser this entire time? Taking Etta to lookouts and infiltrating your way into our lives only to be seeing someone else anyway."

Jamie didn't dare open his mouth. He stood, looking broken, as Skye berated him. And I let it happen because in that moment I wanted him to feel as much pain as I felt.

A pair of headlights cut through the dark of the carpark. "That's us," Skye said. "Come on, Etta. We're going home." She gave Jamie one last withering glare before we slid into the backseat.

It was only then, in the back of the car, that the tears finally came.

I didn't stop crying even when we got to Skye's house. She texted my dad for me on the way back, telling him that I was staying at her house. He messaged back telling me to have fun.

Skye helped me undress in her room, finding me a set of pyjamas to wear and wiping off my smudged makeup. I sat cross-legged on her bed while she brushed out my hair. The bristles running through my scalp soothed me and I closed my eyes, letting out a sigh. Somehow, I stopped crying. I drank water and Skye turned out the light.

That night I dreamt of a snowman and a yellow coat and a phone in a classroom I kept screaming into until my throat dried up. I woke up while the sky was still black. Skye was snoring beside me, her mouth slightly open. For a moment I forgot why I was there and what had happened the night before—and then it all came flooding back in waves of memories. *Jamie,*

Jamie, Jamie. I cried until there were no more tears left.

Skye slept until mid-morning. "Hey," she said, rolling over to find me awake and staring at the ceiling. She rubbed the sleep out of her eyes with the back of her hand. "You're up."

"Yeah," I said.

"Do you want to sleep some more?" she asked. I shook my head. "Breakfast?"

"Water," I said. Skye passed me the water bottle on her nightstand.

After I finished drinking, she said, "Do you want to go home?"

I nodded.

We pulled up to my house an hour later. Skye unbuckled her seatbelt and when I did the same she raised a hand. "Wait one sec," she instructed and left the car before I could ask her why. She went straight around the side of the house and a few minutes later my dad was there to help me out of the car and into his arms. I let him hold me, numb to it all. Skye watched me closely.

It was bad at first; Jamie turned into a fever dream I couldn't stop myself from having. But I knew grief. It was acute in the beginning then a dull ache that slowly ebbed away into something you trained yourself not to feel.

Dad took Jamie's sudden departure from my life with a stoic acceptance. He let me cry on the sofa and brought me tea and tissues. I was glad that Skye had told him what happened. I couldn't bring myself to say it out loud.

Skye looked out for me at school. I dreamt about my mum. In the dreams I was looking down at the kitchen, as if inspecting the crime scene from above. I waited and the phone rang. The backdoor opened and there I was, yellow coat and damp hair from the snow. No matter how hard I tried, though, I couldn't get to the ringing phone.

Time moved forwards as it always did. The sadness continued until it slowly gave way to anger. I didn't want the cards I'd been dealt. I knew I deserved better. I also knew I didn't want to be made immobile by a boy. I'd always made fun of the movies painting out lost love to be the worst feeling in the world. But I understood now. It was grief. I grieved for Jamie, his smell and the taste of his lips. I grieved for the memories of him I could no longer touch. He had stained them with the infidelity.

On the first Saturday of July I woke up before

Dad went to the pool and began moving all of my furniture to the middle of the room. I was sweating by the time I finished, awkwardly propping myself on my bed to open the window. Dad popped his head into my room. "Why are you causing such a raucous—oh." He took in the furniture and the stubborn jut of my chin. "You're on a mission."

"I'm going to paint," I said, hands on my hips and chest heaving. I almost dared him to try and stop me.

Dad nodded. "Just keep it to your room."

I pulled my hair back and changed into an old pair of checkered pyjamas. I got out my acrylics and set to work.

I used almost every paint colour I owned. I mixed and blended, trying to create colours that I'd never seen before. The wall was my canvas and I took to it without fear, pulling my brushes across it in long, free strokes. The early afternoon sun spilled into the room and I rolled up my sleeves. I kept painting.

The colours shifted from shades of dark blue to lilac to pink to bright, fluorescent orange and then white. When I was happy with them, I added small details: a speck of white on emerald eyes, a shadow under the wing. My arms ached but I couldn't feel it properly—I had to keep painting.

I was done by nightfall. Dad came in and surveyed the damage. On my wall was a bird unlike any seen in Cedar. The creature had outstretched multicoloured wings, each feather intricately detailed, and it was standing on a thin tree branch as if ready for flight.

I exhaled. "I just wanted to paint."

"Good," Dad said with an approving nod. "Don't let anyone take that away from you."

In mid-July Dad took me camping. We hiked and canoed and made a campfire in the evenings just like when I was a kid. It was nice to be out on the water or in the mountains where the air was cooler and fresher. We sat under the enormous deciduous trees, our foreheads covered in sweat from hiking, and watched as birds with periwinkle blue feathers swooped by. I slept better in my tent than I had in weeks. We cooked bean stews over the fire and I bathed in the shallows of the river. It reminded me of all the beautiful things I still had in the world. In the mountains I was free from Cedar and everyone who lived there.

Dad said that the first heartbreak was the worst

and second love was the best. I hoped he was right.

Three years ago, we had a snow day in Cedar. I was thirteen at the time and had never experienced a proper snow day before. Schools and most businesses were closed. There was a hum of excitement in our neighbourhood.

Mum was on a business trip. She worked for a charity and was away for weeks sometimes. Dad always made those weeks pass as fast as he could; he knew how much I missed her. I felt like our small family wasn't complete without her saccharine smile or witty comebacks to Dad's dry humour. My parents were made for each other.

Dad said we had to make the most of the snow, a giddy twinkle in his eyes. We wrapped up warm and went out to build a snowman in the garden.

Mum had been gone longer than expected this time. But we didn't talk about it. She said she'd be away for two weeks, but another two passed—and then another. I knew something wasn't right; Dad had been hissing into the phone a few nights earlier. I heard him finish with, "Do it for Etta." He'd closed the door after that but I already felt unsettled.

With gloves on, we started moving snow until

it formed into a small mound good enough to build on. We could have been outside for hours, I wasn't sure. Time became obsolete in the grey outside world. When we were almost ready to start decorating the snowman the ring of the phone resounded from behind the kitchen door.

"I think that's the phone," I said. My cheeks were frozen. Dad opened his mouth to respond. "I'll get it," I said before he could speak. I raced into the kitchen, the warm air jarring after being in the cold for so long. I picked up the phone.

"Hello?"

The line remained quiet but there was static that told me someone was listening. I stayed on the line. I tried to listen for anything in that silence, desperate to make it mean something. "Mum?" I whispered finally, the word breaking as I said it.

The line went dead.

I went back outside. I couldn't feel the cold this time. Dad stood back admiring his snowman efforts. "I think we're ready for the nose and eyes," he greeted me with as the kitchen door slammed shut. "We have some carrots in the fridge—Etta?" Dad's brow furrowed, registering the expression on my face.

I couldn't feel the air reaching my lungs. "She's

not coming back, is she?"

Dad's smile faded. He knew who I meant. "No, sweetie." There was a sadness in his voice I'd never heard before. "Your mum isn't coming home this time."

My leg moved before I knew what was happening. The snowman went down without a fight, snow crumpled into a pile. All of our hard work amounted to nothing. We stood and said nothing. A baby bird cried in the distance. Eventually I began to cry and Dad's warm arms wrapped around me. His grip was tight, keeping me together. "I'm still here. And I'm not going anywhere."

Mum had been having an affair for years. I found out after she left Dad a voicemail on the home answering machine saying that she had a new family in Willow Park, one with a big house and a stepdaughter. I couldn't imagine my dad with his calm demeanour, his simple temperament, begging her to stay. But he said he'd done it for my sake.

It didn't matter how upset we were or how much we tried to ignore the empty seat at the table or the large bags of her clothes Dad hid in the attic. Mum had left us.

Every time I went to Willow Park Gallery I wondered if I would see her there. Would she recognise me? Would she be with her new daughter?

I hoped Mum loved her new and better life. I hoped everyone who had chosen not to have me was happy. Someone had to be. God knew I wasn't.

"I just fucking love this place," Skye declared. I looked around and tried to see what she saw in the plastic seats and fake plants under the fluorescent spotlight. A distant pop song I couldn't make out played in the background and a dad yelled at his three-year-old son running ahead of him to slow down. The toddler looked back at him with a wide grin and chubby cheeks.

"I don't get it," I said. "It's just a…mall."

Skye's hand flew to her chest like I'd just shot her with an arrow. "It's not just a mall. It's a place where dreams are born. This is the place where you can be as materialistic as you want and no one will say otherwise."

I laughed at her. "Skye. Stop being materialistic."

Skye adjusted the bags dangling on her arms, causing the candles she'd bought to clink together. "I have no idea what you're talking about." She was being light, re-enacting the old days when it had just been us. It was a distraction and I was grateful for her attempts. The new rumour in Cedar was Jamie and Joni: the clandestine couple who were apparently having sex in Joni's enormous house. At least, that's what people were saying. I tried not to think about them. When I caught my mind drifting towards thoughts of them together I had to close my eyes and take deep breaths until the nausea left me.

We shopped for another hour until I wanted a sandwich and Skye wanted to go to the bookstore. We planned to split and meet at the bookstore as she usually took a while browsing the art section. I ordered a cheese melt and felt my mind drift.

In my first year of art we had been asked to create a self-portrait. It didn't have to be a physical representation of ourselves. Skye took photographs of her family as they were her blood and her soul. Someone else painted their fears in shades of blue and grey.

I worked with clay back then. I made three pots and painted them with scenes from my childhood: the house, the daffodils Mum planted that shot up in spring, Dad driving with me in the backseat, my legs swinging in the booster seat.

Then I broke the pots. I took them into the empty studio at lunch and screamed as they hit the floor, ricocheting off the tiles in flecks of sapphire, buttercup and copper. I spent the evening gluing them back together so that they formed a wonky but recognisable vase.

When I presented it to my teacher for grading she nodded. "You feel as if you're made up of fragmented pieces but they still come together to make you."

"No. I feel as if I'm made up of what others have left me."

I felt that way now. I thought Jamie had wanted me. I thought Mum had wanted me. Instead, I was left with their broken pieces, trying to form them into something that resembled myself.

I met Skye outside the bookstore and I knew something was wrong. My cheese melt was long gone by that point. I hadn't noticed how hungry I'd been. Skye leapt up from the benches she'd perched herself on as soon as she saw me.

"What?" I said, trying to gauge her expression.

"Nothing," Skye said too quickly. "Are you ready to go?"

I frowned. "I thought you weren't done yet."

Skye waved a hand. "I can come back later."

"Are you sure?"

"Yeah, yeah." Skye began to walk to the exit

and I had no choice but to follow her. She didn't say anything but her eyes kept scanning the people around us as if someone might jump out and attack.

"Skye, what's going on?" I asked in my serious voice.

Skye only shook her head. "It's nothing you need to worry yourself over now."

I let it go and followed her to the bus that would take us home.

Before school started, I returned to the lookout. I wore the cardigan. It was the one Jamie had always pointed out with fondness. Mum had bought the cardigan with me at a thrift shop not long before she'd left. It was the last good memory I had of her. It was the first time I'd worn it in weeks.

Dad offered to drive me to the lookout but I said I'd take the bus. I wanted to be alone in the cooling summer air, the lingering light scattering across the trees in dappled shadows.

I should have known that he'd be there.

There was a shuffle of feet behind me and I knew. I knew.

He appeared older somehow and fuller. Maybe I expected him to be as hollowed out as I felt, but he looked *good*.

An arrow of hurt speared my chest.

Jamie.

"You look like you've seen a ghost," I managed to say.

"I think I have." He stared, unmoving. I was grateful he didn't reach for me. "Why are you here?"

I wanted to say, *Why shouldn't I be here?* Did he really think I would hide from him?

"I like it here."

There was distress in his eyes. I hadn't noticed that before. "Etta—"

"Jamie," I said, cutting him off. I exhaled. "I can't believe this is happening." A laugh I didn't recognise came out. It was cold and closed off.

"I'm sorry. I shouldn't have kissed Joni."

"Which time?"

Jamie shook his head. "I don't know what—I was never with Joni."

"You mean like you're not with Joni now?"

"I'm not with Joni now."

I couldn't look at him while he lied to my face. I clenched my jaw and turned away from Jamie and towards the distant hum of Cedar.

"You don't have to lie anymore, Jamie." I said it softly. I wanted it to be caught by the wind and carried away.

"I'm not lying."

"Yes, you are!" I spun around to face his lies front on. Jamie remained quiet, rendered silent by my hurt. "I just want the truth," I sighed. The weight of resentment was heavy.

"No one was meant to know," said Jamie, his eyes wide and palms open.

"This is Cedar." I said it with as much venom in my voice as I could muster. "Everyone knows everything about everyone."

Jamie began to plead. "I never meant to hurt you. I only ever wanted to be your friend."

"Friends don't kiss like we did."

We were something more.

"I thought you wanted that."

A second arrow of hurt entered my chest and all of my wounds reopened. I gasped for air. "So that's why you did it? Is that why you asked me to the dance, too?" I pressed my lips together to stop myself from sobbing. "Because you thought that I wanted it?"

"No I—"

"I wanted you to want me, Jamie," I said, but my voice faltered, tapering off at the end of the sentence. I could see beyond his expression, beyond the shaking hands at his side. I laughed. "You go along with everything. You came to Willow Park because I did. You sat with us in the art department. You probably kissed Joni that night because you thought she wanted it." My hands were in the air, fury painted all over me, hoping it would disguise my pain. "You do things either because it's easier for you or because you can't be fucked upsetting anyone. Well, Jamie, you hurt me. You fucking hurt me."

Jamie stood, silent. For the first time he truly looked small. I unbuttoned the cardigan and stepped towards him until I could reach out to him. He accepted the cardigan with no response. "I don't need this anymore," I breathed, my chest heaving up and down. "And I don't need you."

Jamie stood facing me until he turned without another word and rode his bike back down the road. I waited at the lookout for an hour so I didn't have to pass him on the long and winding road home. I never wanted to see him again. My heart was still pounding and my eyes stung. But I didn't cry. I didn't scream into the cliffs.

I wanted to move on.

It happened on the last Saturday before school. She was prettier than I remembered. I blinked, the whir of the air conditioning swirling in my ears. I was doing better, able to make it through my shift without bursting into tears. But this was a test I didn't want.

Joni Fraser tucked her hair behind her ears. The store was empty but I hadn't seen her walk in. She wore a tiny white sun dress which emphasised her small frame. She had a basket in her hand, filled with sourdough rolls, camembert, sweet chutney, grapes and sea salt crisps. She at least had the grace to turn deep red and avert her eyes as she walked up to the counter.

It took me a moment to remember I was at work and had no reason to refuse her service. I accepted the basket. The beep of the scanner bounced between us. When everything was in the bag, I stared at her. She frowned. I gestured with a nod of my head to the till. "Price is there."

"Oh." Joni rummaged in her purse and handed me a credit card. I stuck it in the card reader without another word. Her dainty fingers typed in her pin number.

I'd thought about the moment I would see Jamie again but I never imagined seeing Joni. I wanted to yell at her, to scream and tear my own hair out. I wanted her to feel as bad as I did. But I couldn't even say Jamie's name; every time I tried it lodged itself in my throat, suffocating me.

"You're not the only one," I said, almost a whisper.

Joni stopped using the card machine. Her brown eyes widened. "Sorry?"

I could taste the metallic anger on my tongue. "You're not the only one missing a parent."

Joni's face paled. "I...I know," she said in a quiet voice.

"Then why do you act like it?"

"I...I don't mean to."

I bit the inside of my mouth. "Fine."

She looked as if she wanted to say more. Maybe she also had empty words lodged in her throat. She pulled out her card and the machine whirred then printed her receipt. I handed it to her. She didn't take it.

"You won't have to worry about me at school this year," she said.

"I'm not worried," I snapped.

"I mean that I won't be there. I'm leaving Cedar."

I nearly asked her why. "Good."

Joni took the receipt and folded it between her fingers. She reached for her bags. "I'm sorry that your mum left. Perhaps...perhaps we're better off without them."

I didn't want to talk about my mum with her.
I hated that she and everyone else in this town knew
about it. I turned away from her and fiddled with the
buttons on the cash register.

Eventually I heard the automatic doors open
and close. When I glanced at the exit, Joni was gone.

JAMIE

I didn't see her in line behind me.

Mum was making a roast for Christmas dinner even though I told her it was ridiculous to celebrate Christmas two weeks in advance. Mum didn't care. She picked me up from school and we went straight to the grocery store with the fake trees and the reindeer and the stupid tinsel to buy a stupid discount chicken for the dinner.

Mum was so stressed about getting everything in time that she nearly ran her trolley into Joni Fraser—of all people—who was shopping with her dad. Mum began apologising to such a degree that I had to drag her away. I smiled at Joni who tucked her hair behind her ears and returned the gesture shyly.

"Joni is such a pretty girl," Mum said after they were out of earshot.

"She's also very smart," I added. Joni was famous for being the top of nearly all her classes. She took specialist literature, physics, music and maths. People called her Einstein but I think that was only behind her back.

"Doesn't mean she can't be pretty, too," Mum huffed. "You certainly used to think so."

It was common knowledge in my house, and only in my house, that in kindergarten I had been in love with Joni Fraser. It was all because of the nativity play. I'd been a shepherd and Joni had been the angel. She'd been louder back then. I'd been so enchanted by her performance, the way her hands waved around and how she projected her voice to the back of the hall that I had forgotten to say my lines. My sisters teased me about it the entire drive home. Sometimes Nora would still bring it up to get a rise out of me but I had shit on her now so I could hold my own against her.

"Do you spend much time with Joni?" Mum asked, gazing at the tinned tomatoes, probably comparing prices in her head.

"Mum," I groaned.

"It's just a question."

"Can we talk about something else?"

"I thought you liked Joni?"

"Drop it," I warned and Mum raised her hands in defence and said nothing else on the topic.

Thankfully Mum was a fast shopper and had an uncanny ability to find the home brands and discounted items first. Our trolley filled up fast but we still got held up by the line for the till.

I knew my family was discussed among some in Cedar. Three kids, one income and a house with a mortgage that would never be repaid. But they didn't know that Dad was hardly home because he worked every extra hour he could, still hoping for a promotion. They didn't know that Mum applied for jobs nearly every day only to be met with rejection because she had taken too much time off to raise her children. They didn't hear Sam coming home past midnight because she attended bookkeeping classes after work. And they didn't see Nora working every weekend to build her own jewellery business.

Cedar knew nothing about my family.

We finally approached the till after Jacky Carson strutted off without a look in our direction even though Mum knew her well enough to say hello.

Jacky was a gossip. And she liked nothing more than to gossip about us.

When I looked up I saw the girl behind the till. She was from school—everyone was in this town. I think she was in the year below me. Her name badge said *Jeanette* on it. I had a feeling she went by something else but I couldn't remember what. She wore a cream cardigan with a sunflower and she sat behind me in Biology. She was friends with Skye Matthews, the two were inseparable. And her mum had left a few years ago. That's all I knew about her: Biology, groceries, sunflowers, disappearing mother. Not even her last name.

Mum smiled at her. "How are you today?"

"Same old," she said in a sing-song voice. She started packing our bags. "Are you doing a roast tonight?"

Mum smiled in the way she did when she was pleasantly surprised at something she had expected to disappoint her. I was very familiar with this smile. "Yes," said Mum. Then she blabbered on about doing Christmas early and as she spoke I watched Jeanette take in what she was saying.

I snapped back into attention when I realised Mum pointing at me. "I assume you two must know each other from school?" she said as she rifled through the wad of receipts and junk in her bag.

"I'm in the year below. But we have Biology together." Jeanette glanced in my direction and we locked eyes. She had nice eyes, the kind that put you at ease.

"You sit behind me," I said.

"Yeah, I don't really have any friends in the class," she admitted and her cheeks went pink. I didn't think that was embarrassing. She concentrated on punching buttons on the till and Mum pulled out her credit card.

"But do you like the class?" I asked, surprising myself that I was trying to draw out the conversation.

"Not really," she said, and I couldn't help but want to laugh at that. "I just mean that I've had better teachers. I expected more practicals."

"I agree," I said. We stared at each other and neither of us looked away.

"Help me with the bags, please," Mum grumbled and shoved some into my arms. She wanted to get home, I could see it in the stiff angle of her shoulders. I cringed as the receipt printed from the machine with a small whir. I didn't want to know what the final amount was.

I looked at Jeanette. "Nice cardigan," I said then wanted to take it back because who the fuck said that?

"Thanks," she said. We didn't break eye contact. It was intense and honestly a little strange but mostly it made me want to stay and continue talking to her.

"Well that was delightful," Mum cut in. "It was nice speaking with you, Etta." *Etta! That was her nickname!* "Have a lovely Christmas if we don't see you before then."

Etta turned to look at Mum. "Happy Christmas, Mrs Akerman."

"See you in class," I said with a wave.

"Perhaps," she replied.

I helped Mum load the car with our bags. "Well, she certainly likes you," Mum said. She shut the boot with a thud. "Can't imagine why, though."

I couldn't either.

Physical Education was my last lesson of the day on Fridays. It was also when the volleyball team trained, which meant that the class usually disintegrated into a social gathering. We'd taken over the bleachers and I was sitting with Joe while the girls warmed up in front of us.

"She needs to get over it," Lyn groaned and

there were murmurs of agreement from the others. Lyn stretched one leg out on the step above her.

"Her dad left. Big deal. It happens to everyone," Sarah agreed.

I refrained from rolling my eyes. One look around the gym and I knew they were talking about Joni. Apparently she was crying in Miss Stanley's English classroom again. Joni did that a lot since school had started. Whenever she did turn up to sit with us at lunch her eyes were always puffy and her cheeks red. Everyone knew why, and they treated her differently now. It must have been isolating.

Paige nodded fervently, her curly hair bouncing. "Mine left when I was thirteen. You don't hear me going on about it."

"It's pathetic," said Lyn.

"Your dad moved to Willow Park and you still see him every other week," I laughed, but it tasted bitter. "Joni's dad might as well be dead." Everyone stared at me. Joe's jaw slack. It wasn't like me to get involved in any group conflict.

"Does someone have a crush?" Paige mocked. Lyn and Sarah laughed.

I rolled my eyes again and reached down to retie my laces so they couldn't see how my face was heating up.

"I'm tired of talking about this," Joe said, diverting the uneasiness that had fallen upon us. "Besides, Joni's here."

I looked up and Joe was pointing across the gym. Sure enough, Joni was coming out of the changing rooms dressed in her volleyball polo and shorts. I could see the red splotches under her eyes even from the distance.

Our teacher blew the whistle and the girls bounced off to the nets while Joe and I joined our class. I watched as Lyn swept over to Joni and said something to her that turned Joni's face to ice. Lyn smiled victoriously. It made my jaw clench.

My class was supposed to be doing running and training exercises in pairs. Instead, we were running across the gym and chatting to the girls when our teacher wasn't looking. Eventually the girls split into teams and began to train at the tent, forcing us to focus on the exercises we'd been given. I partnered with Joe, wanting to get through the hour so much that I didn't realise half the class had stopped running. Their attention was on the volleyball nets.

"Whoa, look at Joni go," Tom whistled.

"My money's on Lyn," said Jake.

"You're on," Tom challenged.

Joni and Lyn were having what could only be

described as their own volleyball match. The other girls on both sides had stepped back completely, absorbed in Joni and Lyn's one-on-one rally. Even their coach looked baffled.

I watched as Joni spiked the ball over the net with more ferocity than I had ever seen from her. The ball soared over, too powerful for anyone on the other side to hit. It slammed to the floor. There was a split second of silence before Billy whistled and our class applauded her. I clapped my hands together. Joni didn't smile, but there was a triumphant glint in her eye that even I could see from the far side of the gym. She shrugged off the compliments and stared at the net ready for the next round to begin.

Mum glared at me, waiting for my response to something she'd said that we both knew I hadn't been listening to.

"Sure," I said with a flip of my hand, hoping that would pass as an answer. Mum narrowed her eyes and I shoved a spoonful of cornflakes into my mouth. Soft morning light bathed our tiny kitchen in yellow.

Mum had woken up in project mode and was having her usual rant with me about my future, specifically where I should go to university.

"I said," Mum repeated, emphasising each syllable, "you might want to make an appointment with Ms Meyer to talk about funding and scholarships." She picked up the kettle and filled her mug. Steam rose. "You never know. The maths courses you are looking at can be competitive."

We'd already agreed that next year I would take a maths course close to Cedar so I could live at home and learn to be an accountant. "Sure," I said, already knowing that we were given scheduled appointments at school with her next year. That seemed to placate Mum.

At that moment, Nora walked in wearing her silk dressing gown and wet hair wrapped in a pink towel. "Morning," she greeted, not looking at either of us.

"Nora, honey, could you look into a couple of schools with Jamie this weekend? I want him to be prepared when he speaks to Ms Meyer," said Mum.

"I have plans this weekend," I said. No one responded.

Nora opened the fridge and returned with a carton of almond milk. "Ms Meyer goes through that next year," she said.

"I want Jamie to go next week," said Mum.

Nora poured milk into her expensive granola that none of us were allowed to eat and Mum had started making her pay for out of her own money. "What's the rush?"

"I want him to get a head start on it. He'll need to do scholarship applications."

"They won't need to be done for months."

"Could you please do as I ask?"

Nora slammed the cutlery drawer closed and I knew they were about to get into an argument.

I didn't know where I wanted to go to university and I didn't know why I was being pressured to think about it over my cornflakes. I knew I would end up wherever Mum wanted me to go because that was easier than deciding for myself.

Eventually Nora stormed out of the room while Mum was mid-sentence, causing Mum to storm after her, leaving me in peace.

Another week went by of listening to Lyn moan about anything she could think of at lunch. I avoided her and the rest of the volleyball girls during PE, running out of class when the bell went. Billy and Joe caught up with me as we walked across the lawn. They were talking about some party happening tonight at Sarah's house.

"You coming?" Joe asked me.

That's when I saw Etta. She was sitting with Skye Matthews by the busses, her hair in two braids, absorbed in whatever Skye was saying. I hadn't spoken to her at school yet and she'd moved seats in Biology. Maybe I pissed her off at Christmas? I decided in that split moment that I was going over there.

I caught eyes with Etta, who had already been looking at me, and smiled at her before clapping Joe on the shoulder and telling him I'd see him on Monday.

"Hey," Etta called out when I was in earshot. Skye had cast her attention on me, too. I swear she rolled her eyes.

"Jeanette Anderson," I said. I'd looked her full name up in the yearbook over Christmas break. Skye muttered something under her breath. I had the feeling she didn't like me—yet. "You moved in Biology," I said to Etta, sitting down on the wall.

Without missing a beat, she said, "Yeah I moved because there was this huge head in my way and I couldn't see the board."

I chewed my lip to stop my growing smile. "I'll take that. What are you two up to tonight?"

"We're going to an art gallery," said Skye.

"There's no art gallery in Cedar," I said

hesitantly.

"We're taking the train to Willow Park," Etta explained. "There's a great one there and it has this amazing cafe."

"Etta's an artist you know," Skye said.

"I paint. Oils," said Etta.

"That's very impressive. Why are you doing advanced biology then and not art?" I asked.

"Stupidity?" said Etta and I laughed. I noticed that her entire face lit up when I did.

"You think she can't be an artist and a scientist?" Skye clipped. Etta rolled her eyes.

"I'm sure Etta can be whatever she wants," I said.

Skye poked Etta's shoulder. "We better go if we're going to make the train." I waited, a little disappointed that they were leaving. Then Skye looked directly at me and said, "You coming with us or what, Akerman?"

The gallery was special. I felt at peace being surrounded by the white walls decorated with portraits of sad faces and bright splashes of colour. I lost track of time and let Etta and Skye guide me through the maze of art, listening as they talked about the pieces and the people who created them.

"I get why you come here every week," I said to Etta as she showed me a seaside piece with icy blue waters and sharp cliffs. Etta tilted her head and something in her expression made me feel as though she was looking at me and not the painting. I shuffled my feet and looked away. "It's calming."

"It reminds you that there is a world outside of Cedar," Etta said. I nodded. "Have you spotted the hidden figure in the painting?" She took a step closer and I could smell the cotton laundry detergent from her jumper.

"Hidden what?" I asked, my voice uneasy.

"Look." She pointed at the cliffs where a forest trailed off the canvas. I squinted but had no clue what she was talking about. All I could see were speckled trees. Etta inhaled. "It's nice that you're here."

"Why wouldn't I be?"

"Because you didn't know my name until your mum said it."

I cringed and hoped she didn't notice. "Everyone knows everyone in Cedar."

Etta smiled sadly. "I think that everyone believes they know everyone in Cedar from a glance. If we actually stopped to look closer then maybe we'd notice that there are many things not always on the surface."

I stared at the painting, determined to see what Etta saw. And there it was. What I thought was originally a tree was actually a lean androgynous figure, murky and brown, camouflaged in the trees. "I see it!'

"Knew you would," said Etta. Something inside of me warmed. "We'd better go. Skye will be in a mood if they've run out of orange and poppy seed cake while she's waiting for us"

"More of a mood than usual?" I joked.

Etta gave me a playful shove. "She's protective!"

"She doesn't like me," I said.

"Give her a chance."

I threw my hands in the air. "Only if she gives me one."

I followed her out of the rooms and towards the cafe where Skye was waiting with three coffees and three slices of cake.

I'd never spent much time in the art department. When I'd first started Cedar Secondary, art had been compulsory. But I think the whole department was relieved when I finally dropped the subject after my infamous collection of paper-mache people that ended up looking like they belonged in a horror movie.

Yet here I was once again, in the art department, while Etta and Skye worked away. It turned out that Skye was a photographer, and a pretty good one. When we weren't in the thralls of a debate, I would complement her work. Skye had a lot of opinions and I enjoyed playing devil's advocate. She was so smart. I liked to pocket some of her arguments for when I next fought with Nora.

"You should photograph Jamie," Etta joked to Skye one lunch time at the start of February. Skye was showing me photos of a blue weatherboard with an apple tree in the front garden and a makeshift swing hanging from it. It was her old house and for their project to create something from an important memory.

"Very funny," said Skye, not taking her eyes off her laptop, where she was busy editing a photo.

"Have I not made an impact on your life?" I chimed in with pretend shock. "Am I not pretty enough for you?"

Skye pressed her lips together to hide a smile. "Absolutely not."

Etta laughed.

Cedar Secondary was freezing during winter. The old buildings weren't built with insulation; the windows and doors had so many cracks everywhere that the icy air seeped in like water droplets from a cave. In the studio, the windows had frosted over and, despite having the heating turned up, Etta stood painting at the easel with her fingerless rainbow gloves on. She was always getting in trouble because they weren't part of uniform regulations, but she managed to talk her way out of detentions every time.

"Why don't *you* paint Jamie?" Skye asked Etta. I expected her to laugh it off as Skye had done but instead Etta's cheeks flushed pink and then she stabbed at the canvas with her brush.

Skye checked the clock and swore. "I need to go. Can't be late to maths. I'm on my official last warning." She slammed her laptop closed and shoved her books into her bag. Etta didn't move. "I'll see you guys later," Skye called and rushed out of the door, leaving me alone with Etta.

For a while Etta was quiet, continuing to layer paint on her canvas, creating light and shadow in a way that made me yearn to be able to dream something to life. She added an orange she'd meticulously mixed to her canvas with delicate brush strokes. Every so often she'd tilt her head to the side, drawing her brush away from the canvas. If she was happy then she nodded and kept painting. If she wasn't, she pursed her lips and picked up another brush to try something else. The bell eventually rang. We never said a word.

"I'll walk you to class," I said after she finished tidying up.

"Okay."

The hallways were bustling with the usual after-lunch frenzy: the slamming of lockers, the incessant yelling and the scraping of shoes on the linoleum floors. Etta stayed unusually quiet on the way to her locker. My stomach churned. Did I do something wrong?

"Is everything all right?" I asked, suddenly unable not to.

She looked up at me, her wide green eyes blinking. "I'm just thinking," she said, and gave me a smile.

"Thinking about what?"

We reached her locker and I leant to the side as she began to load books into her bag. Her cheeks turned pink again. I waited as she zipped her bag and closed the locker. I couldn't let it go. I wasn't sure why, but I needed to hear her answer.

"I like spending time with you." Etta's voice

was so quiet I almost missed it.

I could've laughed, relief spreading over me. "Well, I like being friends with you, too," I said. Etta smiled, but it didn't meet her eyes.

"Oh. Okay. I'll see you after school," she said, her voice hoarse.

"I thought I was walking you to class."

"Can't have you being late, too," she insisted and started walking away before I could argue further.

People were starting to talk about Etta. There were rustlings in the hallway when we were together, and I caught several people from Etta's year watching me and whispering even when she wasn't around. Still, I'd never been happier. I'd always been popular but for the first time I felt something real with Etta. Even Skye's insults had become softer and were always delivered with a sharp glint of humour in her eyes.

I sat with my old friends at lunch one Wednesday in early March, mostly because Joe kept badgering me about it in PE, but also because Etta and Skye were out for the day on an excursion.

My old friends. I couldn't pinpoint the exact moment that Joe and Billy and the volleyball girls had become people I used to spend time with while Etta and Skye became the people I did spend it with.

When I got to the table everyone fell into a hasty silence. The hairs on the back of my neck prickled. I could hear it in their silence. They'd been talking about me.

Joe smiled and shuffled his tray over so I could take a seat. Lyn was there with Sarah and Paige. The three of them surveyed me with eager eyes. I averted my gaze and realised there was another girl with them. Joni. For a moment I forgot about what they'd been saying about me. Joni didn't look better but she didn't look as if she had been crying all morning. She gave me a small smile.

"Look who's back from the dead," said Lyn. I ignored her.

"How's the art department?" Sarah asked leaning in, ash blonde hair falling in her face as she did. "Or is it who's in the art department I should be asking about?"

"Come off it," I said, stabbing a potato with my plastic fork. Skye had been protesting the use of plastic cutlery in the canteen all year. She'd told me off for it once, claiming that it was killing the planet. "So I have other friends. Big deal."

Lyn folded her arms across her chest. I noticed

in the corner of my eye that Joni was trying to look anywhere but at me and the girls. "I've heard that you've been making more than just friends," Lyn said.

"No idea what you're talking about."

"Of course he's going to say that," Paige cut in. "But the whole school is talking about it. Big shot Jamie Akerman in love with grocery store freak Jeanette Anderson."

I stopped pretending to eat. My knuckles went white around my fork. "She's not a freak," I said cooly. The girls laughed. Joni shifted in her seat still not talking.

"Leave it," Joe warned. "Jamie can and can't date whoever he wants. Stop trying to stir up shit."

Lyn shrugged and I caught Joni's eye. Her mouth twitched like she wanted to say something. She didn't, and when the bell rang she was the first to leave the table.

I stayed at the table long after the others had gone, the conversation replaying over and over in my head.

The whole school is talking about it.

I sifted through every memory we shared. They all felt different now. Etta, pretty with her hair in braids staring at me, lighting up when I walked her to class. Etta sitting next to me in Biology, her body warm and close. Etta's hand on my shoulder when she laughed at something I said. And Skye, who sometimes made excuses to leave us alone.

We could talk about everything together. I felt at ease with Etta. I craved her. I'd told her that she was my best friend and I meant it. But it still didn't feel quite right. Did I want more?

April arrived in tiny pink flowers sprouting in bushes outside school, and longer days spent doing homework in the tiny garden behind my house. That weekend I told Etta I would go with her to a party on the outskirts of Cedar. I was happy to go because I wanted to drink myself stupid. I was confused about my feelings and oblivion called to me.

I convinced Sam to drive me to the party and buy us alcohol. She was always more willing to do this than Nora. Nora would let it hang over me and use it as leverage. With Sam, I just needed to ask nicely and that was the end of it.

The party was at a huge white brick house with black trimmings and a red door. I arrived before Etta and Skye, so I waited on the driveway, gulping wine until Skye's car pulled up and the girls spilled out. I carefully hid the bottle behind my leg in case Skye's dad was driving.

Maybe I was a little drunk or maybe it was the dress, but my jaw dropped when Etta stepped out of the car. She wore a sequinned inky black dress that barely covered her thighs. Her lips were painted a dark red and there was glitter on her eyelids. She met my gaze and I had to look away.

"You drunk already, Jamie?" Skye demanded. Her black hair was pulled to the top of her head. She wore red lipstick and it suited her.

"I'm not sober," I said, my heart, which had been thumping, calming down. I avoided looking at Etta or I knew it would start up again. I got to my feet unsteadily. Maybe I was drunker than I thought.

"Should be an interesting night then," Skye mused and led us up the porch steps towards the front door.

The people at the party were nice. They were mostly girls in the year below, but they welcomed me kindly. Although, judging by the knowing looks they gave me I knew they'd heard the rumours.

I listened as they spoke about their classes. Most of them took art and they discussed the teachers and lack of funding and supplies fervently.

I had nothing to offer these girls. They weren't

like Lyn or Sarah or even Joni. They had opinions on their members of parliament or whether Winona's Wardrobe, the new clothes boutique in town, was truly ethical. I was out of my depth. I drowned my wine too fast, already onto the second bottle in the first hour.

The room began to blur around the edges. My head felt lighter. I started laughing along with everyone, especially at things that shouldn't of been funny. When Etta went to the bathroom, Marigold, the host of the party, leant forward.

"I can't believe I have Jamie Akerman at my party," she said with a saccharine smile.

"Who's he?" I said and everyone laughed. I took a large sip of wine.

Marigold twirled the ends of her hair with her fingertips. "Your sister is Leonora, right?"

"Unfortunately," I agreed and there was more laughter.

"She's a bit of an icon in the Cedar art department," Marigold went on. I blinked at her and when my eyes opened she had two faces. I shook my head trying to clear the double vision.

"She snores," I said. For some reason I flung my arms up in the air, the wine with them. "Like, a lot." The bottle slipped in my fingers.

"Oh no you don't," Skye snapped and Etta— when had Etta returned?—reached out and grabbed it. I pouted at her.

The drunker I got, the more I forgot that other people were at the party and the more I wanted to go outside. I don't know how it happened but I eventually found myself alone with Etta, the others having disappeared somewhere. "All alone," I mused.

"Yes," Etta agreed.

"I want to see the stars," I said abruptly.

"You what?" She laughed at me, her eyes bright.

"The stars, Etta," I said, feeling a sense of urgency inside me. "We have to see the stars."

"All right," she said, still smiling. "We'll go see the stars."

"You're very pretty." I blurted it out. Something in the back of my mind told me I should be embarrassed.

Etta tilted her head to the side. The corners of her mouth twitched but her eyes were solemn. "You're very pretty, too," she said eventually. I exhaled in relief.

We left the room and fluttered outside to the street. I stared at the sky and, to my great disappointment, it was cloudy. There wasn't a star in sight. "The thing about stars," I sighed, trying hard to pronounce every word properly, "is that they are poems we cannot read."

Etta opened her mouth to respond and stopped. "That makes no sense."

"Yeah, that's because I am drunk."

"That you are, Jamie."

I lowered my voice, the words barely coming out. "Am I embarrassing?"

Etta shook her head. "You're hilarious."

"And you're very pretty." There it was again. It was true, and the wine made me want to keep telling her.

"Are you flirting with me?" she asked, looking up at me through her lashes.

The next words fell out of my mouth before I could stop them. "Is it working?"

A pause. The trees rustled and the distant sound of a car in a neighbouring street went by.

"Maybe," said Etta.

I closed my eyes but that made the spinning worse. When I opened them Etta was watching me. "Etta, how come you're not as drunk as me?"

"Because you had a bottle and a half and I had two glasses."

"Oh." I was starting to feel like I might be sick.

Etta's eyes were on me. "I love how you say my name."

I blinked. She really was flirting with me. "Come to the dance with me." Nora had been pestering me about asking someone to go with me for weeks. "Come on!" I pleaded, giving her no time to answer. "It would be fun."

"Okay," Etta laughed, a wild and uncertain expression on her face. "I'll go to the dance with you."

I grinned. The nausea was unbearable now. "Thank you." I pointed at the sky. "And that, everyone, is the poetry of the stars."

The front door swung open and Skye stood in the threshold looking around until she spotted us. "Are you two coming back or what?" she demanded, hands on her hips.

"Jamie needed air," Etta called back.

"Actually I wanted to see the stars," I slurred. Then I threw up. Things were blurry from there.

I ended up sitting on the porch steps with a glass of water Skye had brought me until Sam's headlights pulled up in front of the house. Etta must have called her for me because I didn't even remember picking up my phone.

Sam rolled down the window and stuck her

head out. "Are you going to throw up in my car?" she demanded.

"He should be fine. Just needs to go to bed," Etta answered.

Sam surveyed Etta for a moment longer than I would have liked and then shrugged and told me to get in the car. I got up, and although the world was still spinning I no longer felt the need to empty my guts on the pavement. I waved goodbye to Skye, who sat by the door with a judgmental expression on her face. She grunted back something about a hangover.

I realised that Etta held my arm. She looked up at me. Sam still had her head out of the window. "I had fun tonight," Etta said, her voice low. I could smell her sweet perfume.

"Me, too," I said. "Besides the whole throwing up. Sorry about that." I scratched the back of my head.

Etta reached up and kissed me on the cheek. I froze. "Sleep well," she said and turned to walk up the porch steps. I couldn't make my legs move. Sam yelled at me and finally I got in the car without looking back.

"Well, she likes you," Sam said when we reached the end of the street. She stuck her indicator on even though ours was the only car around.

"I asked her to the dance," I said. The car ride wasn't helping my recovering stomach but I was grateful to have Sam and not Nora driving.

"Do you like her?" Sam said, glancing over at me.

"Yeah, she's my friend."

"Jamie. I think she wants to be more than friends."

"You and all of Cedar Secondary," I muttered.

Sam frowned, eyes back on the road. "So you like her as just a friend and asked her to the dance as just a friend and she kissed you just now even though you're...just a friend?"

"I'm too drunk for this, Sam."

"Just seems weird to me—"

"I'll throw up in your car."

She focused back on the road. "Consider it dropped."

The next day I woke up with a headache and an unsettled stomach. Sam took one look at me in the kitchen and made me eggs, bacon and toast. She slid over a glass of orange juice and told me it would make me feel better. It did.

I kept replaying the events of the night before over and over until they made me dizzy.

Etta talking to me. Etta watching me. Etta

kissing me. Then I would jump to Sam's conversation with me in the car. Then Etta, the kiss, the car. I tried to forget the throwing up part.

Around midday, I drove over to Etta's house. She was on the front steps wearing her cardigan with the sunflower. I loved that cardigan. I waved and rolled down the window.

"Get in the car," I said. Then added, "Only if you want to of course."

"I'm in my pyjamas," she said.

"You're in the same cardigan you always wear. Besides, you don't need to be dressed up for this. You won't even have to leave the car."

Etta paused. "Let me put my mug inside and tell my dad I'm going," she said and went inside.

I scrolled through some group messages while I waited for her. Tom had also had a party last night and they were going on about that, sending photos and drunken videos of each other. I could tell that Joni hadn't been there. I put the phone down when Etta opened the door.

"You ready?" I said with a grin.

"As long as you're not taking me to the woods to kill me."

"Damn. Plan B it is then." We drove out of the suburbs and onto the main roads. Etta asked me how

I was feeling after last night. I screwed my face up. "Sorry about that."

"Don't be sorry. It was fun."

I kept driving. The lookout was my favourite spot in Cedar. Many people didn't like to go there because of the rumours about it being haunted by a jealous divorcée, but I think that's why I liked it. That and the view. I pulled into a parking spot. I unbuckled my seat belt and, like a mirror, she did too.

"I don't remember everything from last night," I said, running my hands over the steering wheel. "I mean I don't know if you know this but I was very drunk."

"Very funny," said Etta, her voice rough.

"I like that cardigan," I said, suddenly aware of how close we were, how she angled her body towards me. Her chest rose and fell and despite the open window, the temperature in the car rose.

"It's pretty old," Etta said. "I should get a new one but I find it hard to let go."

"Then don't."

She didn't look away from me. I remembered calling her pretty last night. I should have called her beautiful, though.

Her lips parted.

I wanted to answer them.

I moved towards her. Etta's lips were soft and her breath smelt of peppermint. The kiss was nice and Etta was nice and I wanted her to be happy.

It turned out that the rumours were true.

Mum caught on to the fact that I hadn't made an appointment with Ms Meyer to discuss universities. "I asked you to do one thing," she snapped at breakfast, slamming the fridge.

"I'm sorry," I said through my mouthful of bran and raisin cereal. "I'll do it today."

Nora walked into the kitchen in her robe. "Morning," she chirped, waving at us.

"I'm angry with you, too," Mum said.

"Wonderful," said Nora.

"You need to sit down with your brother this weekend and go through university options."

"I told you those don't need to be done for—" Mum glared at her and Nora shut her mouth. "Okay we'll go through it on Saturday morning."

It was not the way I wanted to spend my Saturday morning especially as I had exams to study for, but Mum was not to be crossed. Dad had been away for work longer than usual so her temper was shorter than ever.

I was used to Dad being away; it felt more normal than when he was in Cedar. When I was younger, I would cry every time he got out his brown overnight bag, and placed his trousers in neat piles next to the wash bag. The tears wouldn't stop until he pulled me into his arms, his minty breath whispering in my ear, "I won't be away forever, Jamie. When you feel sad, remember that I pinky promise to return." His pinky finger would then wrap around mine and the tears stopped.

Nora and I sat down in the living room on Saturday, right where Mum could see us. Nora pulled up university sites on her laptop.

"This is a waste of time," she said, careful to keep her voice low. She scrolled through to the admissions page. "But here is where you apply for the course and then you click the other link for financial aid. Ms Meyer will talk you through preferences and all of that." She looked up at me. "End of discussion."

"Enlightening," I said drily.

"Now let's talk about the real stuff." Nora waggled her eyebrows. "Word on the street is that Etta's your girlfriend."

"You and the street should mind your own fucking business," I snapped.

"Someone's sensitive," Nora teased, the corners of her mouth twitching upwards.

"I just wish I lived somewhere people didn't care so much about lives that aren't their own."

Nora leant back into the sofa. "You only have to endure it a little longer."

I frowned. "What do you mean?"

"You'll be at university soon—somewhere far away from Cedar and the gossip. Hell, get off this Isle! Go to a big city—Edinburgh or London—you'll love that."

"I'm not leaving Cedar," I laughed. "I'll go to uni an hour away at most and live at home."

Nora sat up. "Jamie, why the fuck would you stay in Cedar?"

"Why do *you* stay in Cedar?" I challenged.

"Because Mum and Dad need me. They need me and Sam until you finish university so we can pay the mortgage."

"Nora—"

"So you might as well make university fun and far away," she interrupted. "I would have loved uni."

"You could still go," I said weakly.

Nora shook her head and the clay toadstool earrings she made for herself swung from side to side. "I didn't get the scholarship for art school, and it was art school or nothing. Instead I worked and built my own business. I'm not bitter, Jamie. I just want you to make the most of what you've been given. Stop settling for the first thing that comes along. And stop trying to please everyone but yourself. No one needs your charity."

"I'm sorry," I said.

Nora rolled her eyes. "Don't be sorry. Do better." A moment passed and Nora sat upright, folding her legs to face me with a worrying mischievous glint in her eyes. "Now," she drawled, "tell me all about your new girlfriend, Etta."

I threw a cushion at her face.

I was nervous the night of the dance. It crept up faster than I expected. Things hadn't changed much with Etta after the kiss. I was certain that Skye knew everything, but other than the usual rumours, no one knew about us. Not really. She hadn't asked me to be her boyfriend. She hadn't asked for anything.

Etta looked like an emerald star in the darkness of the gym. Nora always joked that the yearly Cedar Secondary budget went towards the end of year dance. I think she was probably right. We had terrible heating and infrastructure but a hired out DJ, caterers and two disco balls for the dance.

I asked Etta if she wanted punch and we went over together. I felt a lot of eyes on us and it made me nervous. The punch was spiked with vodka so I poured us small glasses seeing as neither of us were driving, but my spirit still hadn't recovered from the party.

"Etta!" Skye exclaimed from across the gym and Etta ran to meet her, leaving me momentarily alone. It only took a few moments for Joe to materialise beside me.

"Hey, man," he greeted. "Tom put vodka in the punch in case you didn't know."

"Of course he did," I laughed.

Joe looked down. "I see you're here with Etta."

I nodded and took a sip of my drink.

"I think it's nice," he continued. "She seems nice. Maybe you guys could hang with us? Lyn and the other girls are in a good mood."

"I'll ask," I said, watching Etta and Skye swish their dresses and laugh in front of each other. When they came back I suggested sitting with the others. Etta bit her lip with a worried look in her eye, but then Joe swooped in and introduced himself.

"Jamie tells me you're an artist," he said.

I blinked. I'd never told him. It did the trick,

though. Etta's shoulders relaxed, and soon we all gravitated towards the bleachers with the others. I took Etta's hand in my own as we walked over and gave her what I hoped was a reassuring squeeze.

Joe was right about the volleyball girls. They sat with Etta and Skye and introduced themselves with enthusiastic waves of their arms. The only one with a sour look on their face was Lyn, but I was beginning to think that was just a Lyn thing.

Later, I took Etta out onto the dance floor, holding her close to me. She smelt of wildflowers and every look she gifted me was stardust. I liked the moments when I was alone with her most.

"I'm really glad you asked me here tonight," Etta said.

"I'm really glad you said yes."

"I like you a lot," she continued after some hesitation. "You make me really happy."

I didn't know how to reply and her big eyes were looking up at me expectantly. I pulled her closer and hoped she understood. She sank into my embrace. We were both happy in that moment. But maybe we felt it in completely different ways?

Eventually the song ended and we returned to the bleachers with Skye and the rest of the group. Etta joined Skye and began to chat away while I found myself next to Lyn. She stared at me with a coy and infuriating expression.

"What?" I asked bluntly.

"You look nice tonight, Jamie," Lyn slurred. She'd drunk too much punch. "Too nice for Jeanette Anderson."

"Whatever," I said and tried to move away from her.

"Wait." She reached out and gripped my arm. She pulled herself up to whisper in my ear. I could smell her stale breath she'd tried to mask with peppermints. "Joni's in the English classroom. You should go, Jamie. She won't listen to any of us. I know you've always had a soft spot for her."

"You don't know what you're talking about," I said.

"I know that she's there," said Lyn. A sickening smile split across her face. "And I think you care that she's there."

"What the fuck is that supposed to mean?" I demanded. I tried to keep my face still because I could see Etta glancing in our direction. Lyn shrugged before sliding away and turning to Paige, presumably to repeat the same thing.

I dragged my hands through my hair and down my face. I wanted to make sure Joni was okay, but

I didn't want Etta to be alone and I certainly didn't want Lyn to start whispering lies in Etta's ear the moment I left.

But…Joni.

I'd assumed that she hadn't come and the thought of her curled up alone and Lyn taking amusement from it made me feel sick.

I got up and went to Etta. I squeezed her shoulder and said, "I'm just going to use the bathroom—I'll be back." Then, knowing Lyn would be watching, kissed the top of her head.

Miss Stanley's classroom was close to the gym but far enough away that the music was only a white noise in the distance. No one else was around when I got to the classroom. I almost didn't go in because the lights weren't on.

But then I saw her. Joni Fraser sat curled up underneath the whiteboard. Her shoulders were shaking. I pushed the door open. Joni's tear-stained face snapped up as she sensed my movements.

"Jamie?" Her voice came out hoarse.

"Are you okay?" I asked and then regretted saying it because of course she wasn't.

Joni continued to cry, her knees pulled tight to her chest, arms around them. It looked like she was trying to hold herself together.

I knelt before her and waited because that's all I could do. My mum would say that Joni needed to cry it out so I let her.

"I'm sorry," she said when the hysterics had died down and there was only the residue of silent tears on her cheeks. She looked at me and half of her makeup was smeared across her face. Instinctively, I reached out and rubbed it off with my thumb. I was gentle. Her skin was soft and damp.

She was beautiful, Joni. Her brown skin that was almost gold. Black hair that hung sleek past her shoulders. She'd left it out even for the dance. She always left it out.

"I'm sorry," she repeated. "I have a lot going on at the moment."

"Yeah, I know," I said. Her eyes widened. "I mean, I heard. I'm sorry."

"I suppose everyone is talking about it," she said.

"No," I said instinctively. Joni gave me a disbelieving look. "I mean yes. Not everyone. Some people. They're all on about how Gemma keyed Rhys's car last week. Apparently he was cheating on her with some girl from Willow Park."

Joni choked out a laugh. "Good for Gemma."

I wrung my hands together, desperate for

something else to say or do that would actually make a difference and not make me look like a moron.

"I…er…I like your dress."

Joni raised one eyebrow and I held in a laugh. "I bought it at the last minute," she said, smoothing out the pale blue fabric. "I wasn't sure if I should come but then I didn't want to be in the house alone again so I did." She inhaled sharply. "It was just all too much when I got here. It's not just that I'm sad— it's overwhelming to have everyone talking about you. And Lyn is—"

"A bitch," I finished.

"Yeah." Joni wiped at her face. "It's good that you don't sit with us anymore. I mean, I miss seeing you at lunch, but I think you're better off spending time with other people. We're not the nicest group."

"You're nice," I said, the words falling out of my mouth.

Joni clasped her hands together. "I suppose I'd better leave. I'm a mess and can't bear the thought of spending the evening with Lyn."

"Would you like a hug?" I blurted out.

She laughed again but nodded and I pulled myself towards her and then embraced her. Joni was fragile in my arms and I didn't squeeze too tight for fear of breaking her.

The dance seemed lifetimes away. I felt as if I had always been here with Joni. We drew back and hesitated. It was the hesitation. That was the catalyst. She stared at my eyes and then the briefest flicker to my lips.

But I did it.

I was the one who answered that minuscule thought with my own lips pressed to Joni's in a kiss.

And that's when I heard the classroom door click open.

Joni pushed me back with her hand. Thinking she wanted to stop, I scooted back on my hands and a flash of green fabric caught the corner of my eye. I stared up at Etta. She stared back at us, unblinking, her mouth open but with no words coming out. The usual twinkle in her eyes was gone.

Dread flooded me and my senses blurred together. I couldn't see properly. My brain shut down.

"What the fuck?" Etta whispered. She backed unsteadily out of the room.

"Shit," I said and pulled myself to my feet. "Shit. Etta, I'm sorry. It's not—well it is—what you think. I—"

She was already down the hallway, disappearing into the gym. I didn't want to run and make a scene but I also didn't want her to leave without getting to explain. She wasn't in the gym when I got there. Neither was Skye. I passed my friends who called out to me to join them. I made my way into the foyer and then outside to the carpark.

They were the only people out there. Skye had a phone clasped in her hand, Etta wrapped around the other.

"Etta," I called out. She flinched away from me and a stab of pain shot through my chest. "I'm so sorry," I went on. "Please let me explain."

Skye stepped between us without missing a beat. "You need to fucking stay away."

I froze. "She was upset," I pleaded to Etta. "I shouldn't have done that. I'm so sorry. I didn't mean to."

Skye whirled on me. "Oh, it just happened, did it? Tell me, Jamie, have you been fucking Joni Fraser this entire time? Taking Etta out to lookouts and infiltrating your way into our lives only to be seeing someone else anyway."

I couldn't speak. I just watched as Etta hardly looked at me and a pair of headlights rolled into the carpark. "That's us," said Skye. "Come on, Etta. We're going home." She glared at me and put one hand on Etta's back, guiding her to the car. The door slammed shut.

The car screeched out of the carpark, leaving me standing in the cold.

The gym doors reopened and a group of girls from the year below me stumbled out, giggling with each other, clearly drunk from the punch. I envied their easiness, the fun they were having.

Etta, Etta, Etta.

I thought about racing to her house and standing outside, demanding that she listened to my apology. I wanted to reverse time and never ask her to the dance in the first place. I wanted to have never taken her to the lookout. I wanted my friend back. I put my head in my hands.

What had I done?

I tried to make it up with Etta but she wouldn't even look in my direction. Skye became her personal bodyguard and stopped me from getting anywhere near them.

I watched as she changed seats in Biology to the opposite end of the room. I went straight home after school on Fridays. I sat with Joe at lunch. The girls were there too but we made an effort to sit as far away from them as possible. We migrated to the lawn as the weather warmed, drinking in the sun after winter.

Joni stopped sitting with anyone at lunch altogether. Word was that she'd started going to the library. I tried not to look at her on Friday afternoons in the gym.

Mum knew something was going on with me. She asked repeatedly but I told her I didn't want to talk about it.

Summer didn't arrive soon enough. I spent the start of the holidays with Joe at his house in the pool or riding around Cedar on my bike.

Dad worked even longer hours during the summer months so Mum was catching trains across the country to visit him whenever she could. She always left Sam in charge, which was bullshit because Sam only ever bossed me around and let Nora get away with whatever she wanted.

"I'm throwing a party this afternoon," Nora told me at breakfast one morning in late July. We were in the middle of the annual Cedar heatwave and the house felt like an oven.

"I'm sorry but aren't you meant to ask me first?" I demanded.

"I asked Sam," Nora said. Sam stood by the toaster waiting for her bagel, ignoring both of us.

"I don't like crowds," I lied.

"Since when?"

"Since always."

"Don't be a dick," snapped Nora.

"Sam, what do you really think about this?" I demanded.

Sam shrugged. "I'm going to the movies and no you can't come. I have a date."

"Ha!" Nora yelled victoriously.

"Fuck you both," I muttered under my breath, but neither of them heard or, more likely, neither of them cared.

I got ready and went out for a bike ride. I knew all the streets of Cedar and loved the way it was almost like I could launch off the ground and fly if I peddled fast enough. I never cycled near Etta's house. I'd done it once, and it had left me shaking and breathing heavily. I was careful after that.

I was out the entire morning. The air stuck to my skin. I hated the humidity but it usually meant a storm was brewing and that would mean the end of the heatwave.

It got to the afternoon and I was sweating from the cycle. I pulled into the carpark behind the mall and ran into the supermarket section, returning with two ice creams and a bottle of water. I sat in front of the doors, enjoying the occasional rush of air conditioning whenever anyone walked through them. I ate my chocolate ice cream and then the toffee one, scrolling through my phone but not taking any of it in. When I finished, the sky was black and the sun nowhere to be seen.

It started to shower by the time I unlocked my bike, rain cascading over everything. It felt like little bullets exploding against my skin, leaving me numb all over.

I laughed.

I laughed and threw my hands out, spinning around. I couldn't explain what I felt, but it was the first emotion I had experienced in a long time that didn't stab into my open wounds. I was free.

In the distance I heard my name being called. I don't know how long they'd been calling it for. I turned and some part of me wasn't surprised.

Joni Fraser pulled up beside me in her silver Land Rover. Water dripped down my face. I shook my hair back. "Isn't this amazing?" I shouted. A shudder of thunder split the distance. It thrilled me.

"Get in!" Joni yelled over the rain. "I'll drive you home."

"I have my bike," I said. "I can just ride." The rain was intensifying, if that was even possible. The thunder crept closer. Joni said something else but

I didn't hear her. The storm welcomed me into her volatile arms and I gladly walked into them.

"Get in the car!"

Joni's voice cut through the storm. There was determination in the clench of her jaw and fear in her dark eyes. Without a second thought I got in the car. I shut the door and the world went quiet. The car was much nicer than any I'd been in. It had black leather seats and the dashboard was digital. I was suddenly very aware that I was soaking wet, dripping all over the nice interior. I shuffled my feet.

"What about your bike?" asked Joni.

"Oh." I'd forgotten about my bike. "Yeah I'd better get that." Joni opened the boot from inside and I ran back out and got my bike.

"Where's your house?" said Joni, as I clambered back in the car.

"Behind the school. But I can't go there."

"Why not?"

I made a face. "My sister's having a party and I don't feel like dealing with drunk people right now." I went on, trying to fill the silence between us. Was she thinking about the last time we were alone together? "Why are you hiding out at the mall? Isn't Paige having a girls only gathering or some shit like that today?"

The rain was relentless outside. It was so loud against the roof of the car I could barely hear my own thoughts.

Joni bit her lip, her eyes glistened and I realised with horror that she was on the verge of tears. "Fair enough," I said, "You'd probably have more fun here anyway." Joni remained quiet. I lowered my voice. "Are you okay?"

"I used to hate it when Ellie had parties in the summer." Her voice was soft.

I blinked, puzzled. "Who?"

"My sister," she said. I could have kicked myself for being so stupid. I knew Ellie—she had a reputation for chewing through most of the boys in the older years. Joni began telling me all about Ellie being abroad for summer. I waited for her to stop but she kept going ang going. "What?" Joni stopped speaking and tugged at her hair.

"I don't think I've ever heard you talk that much. Ever."

She bristled. "I do talk." Her gaze fixed on a spot in the distance and I longed to know where her thoughts had trailed off to. "I do talk," she said again, her tone fiercer. "Most of the time people aren't listening to me." I wanted to reach out to her—to just hold her—but she put the car into drive and started moving.

The rain had ceased enough that she could have let me out to ride home, but she didn't. Joni drove us out of the carpark and onto the main road. I had no idea where we were going but when we pulled into a paved driveway with a red brick house standing tall at the end of it, I knew. Joni parked the car and we got out in silence.

"Do you want a drink?" she asked as she unlocked the door. The inside of Joni's house was just as spectacular as the outside. A giant staircase stood in the entranceway with a mezzanine looking down on us. Everything was clean and the house smelt of fresh cotton. There was even a sparkling chandelier hanging from the high ceilings.

My mum would have loved this house. I was filled with a sudden cascading wave of sadness. I wanted my mum to have something like this but I didn't want her to feel like her life had been a failure just because we didn't live in a house with a pool and every new kitchen appliance available.

In the kitchen, Joni handed me a can of lemonade and poured herself a glass of ruby red cordial. She gestured to the sofas across the open-plan room and I went over, hesitant to sit because I was soaking wet and her house was basically a palace.

"I didn't know you were rich," I said. It was meant to come out light-hearted but instead the words were harsh and cutting. She probably thought I was jealous. I added, "You're never coming over to mine, you'll think it's the guest house or something." It was meant to make her laugh, but she didn't.

"We're not rich." She tucked her hair behind her ears.

"You have one of those taps that does boiling water."

"My grandma bought us this house," she said. "She put that in."

"Okay." I decided to sit down anyway, putting the lemonade on the fancy glass coffee table. Joni continued to stand.

"Do you want to change?" she asked. It sounded a little like she was trying to get me naked, which at once amused and also terrified me. "I mean because your clothes are wet," she clarified.

"I'm good," I said, although I was starting to get very uncomfortable wearing wet socks. "But thanks." She remained standing, not quite meeting my eye. I thought about leaving, but I didn't. Joni drew me in with some power I couldn't explain. "Are you—er going to sit down?"

"Okay," she said, and went to sit opposite me. I was certain that she was trying to look anywhere but in my direction.

I fixed my gaze on the shelf of framed photos next to me, hoping it would help relieve her obvious anxiety. The shelf was one of the few personal touches in the immaculate house. Most of the photos were of Joni and a girl close in age I assumed was Ellie. They looked alike but I could tell in each of them which one of the girls was Joni. Joni, even as a kid, had an introspective glint in her eyes. She looked as if she could read your mind but chose to keep your secrets anyway.

I cleared my throat. "Do you ever think about the dance?"

"The dance?" she repeated. I could only nod my head. She closed her eyes, long lashes brushing her cheekbones. I shuffled forward, waiting. Joni's eyes fluttered open. "Yeah, I'm sorry about that."

"It definitely wasn't your fault," I assured her.

"I didn't know that you and—"

"We weren't," I interrupted. I couldn't hear Joni say Etta's name out loud. I rubbed the back of my neck. "Nothing official. Just friends. Well, used to be. Either way…it's not your fault. I'm sorry."

After a moment, Joni asked, "Do you mind if I

light some candles?"

I stopped my rambling. She'd changed the conversation so easily that I felt like we'd been talking about candles all along.

"Sure," I said slowly and she disappeared, returning with a box of matches in one hand.

"Are they scented?" I asked. "My sisters are obsessed with scented candles—Mum too. The house smells permanently like vanilla or caramel or something. It's nice but just a bit much." I was forever opening windows trying to get the overwhelming smell out of the house.

Joni pulled a jar from the mantlepiece and stuck it in my face. The scent was like being at the ocean. I could almost hear the waves and feel the salt on my skin. I could see colourful beach huts and rusted hinges and seagulls swooping in the distance.

"That's actually nice," I said. I looked up and our eyes met. I felt at once like we were both in the middle of the ocean clinging onto each other, hoping to make it out but not trying to swim to shore. "What is it?" I asked, praying that my voice sounded steady.

"It's called Oceania," said Joni. She lit the candle with the crack of a match. "It smells like being on holiday at the beach. Balmy summer evenings, salt water, sleeping easy. My Grandma has a house on the cliffs that overlooks the sea. I loved going there as a kid but we haven't been back much recently." I watched her, transfixed by her words and how generous she was with these stories. My face felt like it was on fire. "I sleep better by the sea."

She sat back on the sofa. It was still raining outside, the water splashing against the windows and the paved exterior of the garden. Joni was right. She did talk and we were idiots, fools, for not listening to her.

"Are you sure you don't want to change?" Joni asked in a low voice. She said something about clothes from one of Ellie's boyfriends but I didn't hear her. The hairs on my arms tingled and my heart sped up.

I got to my feet and joined her on the sofa. Her breaths became heavier. We looked at each other and I swear we both saw something in each other's eyes that we weren't able to name. I placed my hand gently behind her neck. Her skin was warm.

"Is this okay?"

"Yes," she whispered, and I pressed my lips against her's.

The kiss was gentle; it should have been our first.

Her lips were soft and tasted like vanilla. My

head felt light as I tried to comprehend what was happening. I kissed her harder. We continued in this way until Joni's hands latched onto the hem of my t-shirt and I went hot all over.

Her mouth became hungry and she pushed me backwards onto the sofa, her legs on either side of my body. I pulled Joni closer, desperate for every part of her. She took my t-shirt off.

"Have you?" I asked as we paused for air. I was suddenly embarrassed to ask the question; aware of my bare chest between us.

"No," she said. "Never. You?"

I shook my head, still unable to find my voice.

"Should we go to my room?"

God, I wanted that more than anything else.

"Is that what you want?" I asked.

She stared at me with her brown eyes that were speckled with gold up close. She had a dark spot on her left cheek bone. "Yes," she said and I exhaled deeply. Joni rose, one hand outstretched, and took me to her room.

The rain continued to fall outside, the air cooling and the heatwave finally broken.

Being with Joni was like learning to breathe

underwater. I let the events of the year fade away into nothing, burying all my mistakes and vowing never to bring them back from the grave.

I spent nearly every day with Joni. I liked listening to her talk, probably because I wasn't used to it, and some twisted part of me thought that it made me special. She opened up slowly, unfurling like a flower in spring. I drank in each of her words and found that through them my own world appeared brighter.

It was a balmy afternoon at the start of August. The sun glared down from the sky. Joni wore a pale blue bikini that shone in the sunlight. We swam around the enormous pool in her garden, our quiet splashes the only sounds that could be heard. It was always quiet at Joni's house. Her neighbours weren't stacked on top of her house like they were on my street. It made me feel like I was in a different world.

"Do you want something to drink?" Joni asked. Her wet hair clung to her face and neck. I nodded and she got out of the pool. Her bathers stuck to her body. The back of my throat ached with desire.

Joni returned five minutes later holding up a bottle of white wine. "Ellie's stash," she explained and unscrewed the lid with a small snap. "I'd say we could take some from the cellar but my mum already has." She took a swig and then passed me the bottle and I did the same. The wine was sweet.

"It's probably irresponsible to drink when we're around water," I said, wiping my mouth with the back of my hand.

Joni jumped into the pool, splashing water over the sides. She emerged at the surface and swam over to me. She reached her arm out. I handed over the bottle then drifted over to her and guided her body so she could wrap her legs around my waist. She drank and then put the bottle on the side. Joni gazed down at me, her lips parted.

"I'm glad it's summer," she said. Water brushed her eyelashes, drops speckled her cheeks.

"Me, too."

She brought her lips down to meet mine and we didn't talk again until we were out of the pool, showered and lying on her bed, Joni's head resting in the crook of my arm.

"Tell me about the beach," I said.

She laughed. "Why?"

"Because you have candles that smell like it and shells in every corner of your room and you seem lighter when you talk about the ocean." The last part came out by mistake. She stared at me. "Come on," I nudged her. "I want to hear about the beach."

"Mum and Dad would take us to stay with my grandma during the summer when we were kids," Joni said hesitantly. "I loved going orca watching." Her eyes found a spot in the distance as if she could see the memories she spoke of playing out on her bedroom wall. "Ellie liked the rock pools. We drove our parents mad when we didn't wash our feet properly and woke up with sand in our beds. Ellie's nose always got sunburnt. I tanned." I traced patterns on her bare stomach as she spoke. It was mesmerising, like hearing an old story I'd heard before in another life. "The air tastes of salt. It's the only place I've ever felt safe."

I felt Joni's tears before I saw them. They dropped down on my arm in tiny splashes. "Are you okay?" I asked gently. She cried even more and then she said she was fine and wiped her face, but it was only getting worse. She tried to push me away. I held on. I held onto Joni; my lifejacket in the middle of the ocean. I let her cry until eventually she fell asleep.

I stayed with her and then made sure she had something to eat before I kissed her and said I would be back the next day.

Nora was in her room when I got home. I went straight up and knocked on the open door. She heard me but didn't look up. "Nora," I said warily.

"No," she said.

"Please," I insisted.

"I'm working."

"Well, it has to do with that."

She still didn't look up. "What do you want?"

"Do you have anything with orcas?"

Nora continued her painting. "I don't work for free."

"I could pay you," I said, drumming my hands on the table. I had some money saved from my last birthday.

Nora set her paintbrush down, took off her glasses and turned to look at me. There were little red marks on the bridge of her nose where the frames had been digging into her. She considered me for a moment. "I might have something. I will let you have it free of charge."

I didn't leap at the generosity. Nora was not the generous sister; she was hard-edged and strategic and she always wanted something from you in return. Dad called her "No Favours Nora".

"What do you want from me in return?" I asked.

"You have to tell me who it's for." I almost walked out of the room right then. Nora smiled victoriously. "Sam seems to think you're hooking up with someone and lying about it. I want to know before she does."

"So you can hold it over her," I said.

Nora shrugged. "No orca then." She picked up her paintbrush.

"Fine," I said and she stopped. "But you have to keep it between us. No telling Sam or anyone."

"Deal."

I shut the door then took a deep breath. "It's for Joni Fraser."

Nora's jaw dropped. "Get out."

"You promised not to tell."

Nora waved her hands around impatiently. "Does it look like I'm telling anyone?" She narrowed her eyes. "Is that where you've been all day?"

"That wasn't part of the deal," I said flatly.

Nora paused. "Are you lying?"

"I'm not lying," I said, and something in my tone must have convinced her.

Nora leant back in her chair. Finally, she said, "When do you need it by?"

"As soon as possible."

"You'll have it tomorrow morning," said Nora.

"It doesn't have to be—"

Nora waved me off with her paint-stained hand. "Go. I need to work."

Nora was true to her word, and the next morning I found a gift bag filled with tissue paper outside my room. Inside was a clay orca painted black and white on a silver chain, with *Joni* written on the belly.

I brought the orca necklace to Joni after breakfast and I only realised how nervous I was when I rang the doorbell.

"What's that?" she asked when we were in the kitchen, eyeing the bag.

"Go ahead and open it," I said, trying to give her a confident smile.

"What is it?" she repeated, not moving.

I rolled my eyes. "Just open it."

Joni shuffled through the tissue paper apprehensively before pulling out the necklace. She stared down at it, her expression unreadable. "Do you like it?" I asked, hoping she couldn't sense my anxiety. "My sister makes them."

Joni turned the orca over, studying it. She hesitated when she read her name on the belly. "You didn't have to get me anything."

"I know I didn't have to. I wanted to."

We went upstairs and Joni faced the mirror while I moved her hair to the side and clasped the necklace around her neck. I wrapped my arms around her waist and we stared at each other in the mirror. The necklace was perfect.

Joni began to undress me and I the same to her. My fingers caught on the buttons of her top and she helped me.

God, she felt so good. It felt so good being with her.

I learnt a lot about Joni over the weeks. I learnt her body, but also learnt that she loved vanilla ice cream and tucked her hair behind her ears when she was nervous. I learnt, through casual comments, that her mum was an alcoholic. I learnt that Joni missed her sister but not as much as she missed her dad.

One afternoon we searched the house for a photo she claimed was missing from the living room. Joni wasn't herself. She darted around the house, not caring about the mess she made as she searched.

"What is it about this photo?" I joked with a cushion in my hand, as if a photo frame would be hidden in a sofa.

"We're not having sex until we find it," Joni said.

I laughed, thinking she'd made a joke but one look at her clenched mouth and I went back to searching.

We spent hours looking but with no luck. Joni's shoulders sagged and I knew that I needed to make her laugh. I wrapped my arms around her and pulled both of us onto the sofa. Joni gasped and then began to cry out in laughter as I tickled her belly.

"Jamie! How did you know I was—no more!" I stopped and she lay back in my arms, her chest rising and falling, heart thundering underneath. I laughed at the incredulous look on her face and kissed the top of her head.

After a moment, I decided to ask the question that had been on my mind all morning. "Do you miss him?"

Joni's breath hitched. "He left in the night. No goodbye. No note. Not even a voicemail. The day after Christmas."

Hurt pierced me. I wanted to hold her closer. "I'm sorry."

"Worse things have happened to people."

I blinked. "Doesn't make it easier. School must have been difficult after that." I paused. "You weren't—yourself," he finished.

"I didn't have anyone to talk to."

I nodded. Lyn and the other girls were too busy talking about her behind her back. "No one deserves that," I assured her. I ran my hand through her soft hair. "We'll find the photo." Then I added, "We might have to break your no sex rule though."

Joni laughed.

"What happened to Etta?" Sam asked as I was setting off to Joni's place. I was mid-way through packing my rucksack on the kitchen counter. My heart stopped at the mention of Etta's name. It's not as if I hadn't thought about Etta. She lived in the back of my head constantly. She was just a topic that was easy to push aside. I didn't have to think about Etta while I had Joni.

"What?" I said. Pretending I didn't hear her was my safest bet.

Sam sipped her morning coffee. "You never talk about her anymore. Then there's the rumours about the dance."

I whipped around. "What rumours?"

"About how Etta left the dance in tears because of something terrible her date did in an English classroom."

A lump formed in my throat. "Where did you hear that?"

"Everyone knows about it," Sam said. "You've

just been too busy with that other girl to realise."

"Don't be a gossip," I said coldly. "Aren't you too old to care about this?"

"Don't fuck with people because you can't make up your mind about something," Sam shot back.

I left without another word.

The day was ruined. Even Joni couldn't make me feel better. I tried to be what she wanted, yearned to please her.

I agreed to go to a party with her and I knew from her delicate smile that she had nervous to ask me, expecting rejection. I avoided her gaze so she wouldn't see the guilt plastered on my face.

We had burgers for lunch and, high on the feeling of pleasing her, I mentioned going to the beach before the end of summer in the hope that getting out of Cedar would help me to escape my own head.

"We could stay in the beach house," Joni said.

"Is that where you take all your boyfriends?" I had wanted to make a joke but failed.

"I don't have any ex-boyfriends," she said with a shake of her head. "You know that."

"Neither do I," I said, feigning lightness. "Nor ex-girlfriends for that matter." I wanted to change the subject.

"What about Etta?"

Everything blurred. I put down my burger. "What about Etta?" I tried to ask nonchalantly. I knew it didn't come out that way.

"I just…I just thought you were…because of the dance." Joni fiddled with a corner of her bun she had picked off. I'm sorry."

"I haven't been friends with Etta since the night of the dance," I said briskly. "She was never my girlfriend." I got up, suddenly not hungry and feeling itchy under my skin. I needed to get away.

"Where are you going?" asked Joni meekly.

"I forgot I have to run an errand for my mum," I said, grabbing my backpack. We both knew it was a lie. Then I kissed Joni's forehead, hoping to soften the blow. "I think it might run late so I can't come tonight. You have fun, though. I'll see you later."

I didn't know where to go, so I rode my bike to the lookout. There was someone already there when I arrived. They had their back to me as they looked out over Cedar. Hearing my bike on the gravel, they turned around.

My mouth dried up.

She wore the sunflower cardigan, and her hair had grown longer than ever.

"You look like you've seen a ghost," Etta greeted me. I couldn't read the expression in her green eyes.

"I think I have," I managed. I didn't dare move. "Why are you here?"

"I like it here."

"Etta—"

"Jamie."

The air kept still between us, building an invisible wall. I had things to say to her but I couldn't think of any of them.

"I can't believe this is happening," Etta laughed. It wasn't the laugh I was used to. This was a sharp sound that cut me down.

"I'm sorry. I shouldn't have kissed Joni."

"Which time?"

I shook my head. "I don't know what—I was never with Joni."

"You mean like you're not with Joni now?"

"I'm not with Joni now," I said. I was a coward.

Etta spun around to stare out towards Cedar. "You don't have to lie anymore, Jamie."

"I'm not lying."

"Yes, you are!" Etta snapped and turned back to face me. Her face had hardened. Her soft cheeks were now defined by stiff lines and her jaw was set. "I just want the truth."

"No one was meant to know," I whispered.

"This is Cedar," Etta spat. "Everyone knows everything about everyone."

"I never meant to hurt you. I only ever wanted to be your friend."

"Friends don't kiss like we did."

"I thought you wanted that."

Etta's eyes widened. "So that's why you did it? Is that why you asked me to the dance, too?" Her face twisted into disgust. "Because you thought that I wanted it?"

"No I—"

"I wanted you to want me, Jamie," Etta said, and for the first time I saw the cracks in her icy facade. She was in pain. "You go along with everything. You came to Willow Park because I did. You sat with us in the art department. You probably kissed Joni that night because you thought she wanted it." She threw her hands in the air. "You do things either because it's easier for you or because you can't be fucked upsetting anyone. Well, Jamie, you hurt me. You fucking hurt me."

I had nothing to say. She unbuttoned her cardigan and walked close enough to reach out to me. She gave me the cardigan. "I don't need this anymore," she said. "And I don't need you."

I couldn't remember riding home. All I could see and hear and breathe was Etta. I threw up on the side of the road, the conversation playing in my head. I couldn't turn it off. I had Joni, but it was so I might forget about Etta. I couldn't do anything right because whatever I chose hurt one of them. I clung to the cardigan until I was okay to ride home.

When I got to my house I threw the cardigan in the backseat of the car. Best to keep it hidden from my sisters. Inside was quiet as I crept upstairs, ready to pass out.

When I was ten, I broke my mum's antique vase. I was playing with a tennis ball inside against her wishes. The vase fell in slow motion and then shattered into millions of shiny pieces when it hit the ground. Mum ran from the kitchen after hearing the crash and I'll never forget the look on her face. Relief at first because I was okay, and then immeasurable grief. I cried until she held me and told me it would be okay. But I knew I had broken something beautiful that I couldn't repair.

I woke up the next morning feeling hungover. Dread filled my stomach but I knew I had to end things with Joni.

If Etta didn't need me then Joni sure as hell didn't either. I realised that I could drag her through hell and she would still smile and thank me. She deserved better.

I borrowed the car and drove to Joni's house after breakfast. She was outside as soon as I pulled up. Her hair was damp and up close she had dark circles under her eyes. How long had it been since she'd slept? How long had I not noticed?

Joni went in to get her shoes, wanting to come out with me. When she got in the car, I unbuckled my seatbelt and embraced her. She gasped but sank into my arms. It took everything in me to let her go.

"I'm sorry I snapped at you yesterday," I said as I released her.

"It's okay."

I started driving. I took us to the lookout; it was the only place on my mind. I parked and then rolled down the window so the cool air cleared my mind. I knew what I had to do but I didn't want to do it.

"I think we should talk about the dance," I said. I willed myself to stay calm.

"We don't have to," Joni said too fast. She folded and refolded her hands. "I'm sorry I made it weird yesterday."

"I don't want you to be sorry. I want to explain."

"Okay."

"I shouldn't have kissed you the night of the dance."

"I know," said Joni.

"I went to the dance with…but when I found you—"

"It's okay," Joni said for the third time. "I understand."

She wouldn't let me finish. I needed to explain to her that we shouldn't be together—not that I didn't want to. I ran a hand through my hair. "I'm fucking this up so bad."

Then I saw it, sitting in plain sight from my rearview mirror.

The sunflower.

Yellow and bright and cheerfully mocking, stitched onto a cardigan that wasn't mine but was on the backseat of my car. I couldn't hide my horror. The car felt too hot despite the open window. Joni followed my gaze.

I had thought that Etta walking into the English classroom at the dance had been the worst thing to happen. This was worse.

"Joni," I croaked. "It's not what you think."

She unbuckled her seatbelt and, with her head high, unlatched the door.

"No! Joni. Please."

She kept going and going until she turned the corner onto the road. Would she walk all the way home just to get away from me?

I wanted to run after her, tell her I was stupid. I didn't. I just watched the empty carpark, not daring to hope that she might come back.

When I reached up to rub my face my hands came away wet. When did I start crying?

I missed her already. I missed the crunching ice cubes from the cordial she drank between her teeth. I missed the lush smile that would grow from her lips to her cheeks, dimples deepening, when she woke up from a nap. Joni was made up of the ocean; she was as consistent but enticing as the tide.

I'd broken Etta and now Joni. Both would have scars drawn by my hand. I owed them everything but had nothing left to give. I was the ghost at the lookout, stumbling around trying to grasp onto something real. I was a cardboard cutout of all I hated about Cedar.

I don't know how long I cried for. It was dark when I drove home. Mum was in the living room—I'd forgotten she got back that afternoon.

"James, what's wrong?" she asked, taking one look at me. Concern made its way onto her already lined forehead. She put down her magazine.

"I'm okay," I managed to say before the tears came back. Somehow Mum got me sitting next to her.

"Cry it out," she whispered and stroked my head as my body rocked with relentless waves of grief and guilt.

Somehow, I told Mum everything from the very beginning. "What do I do?" I asked after I'd finished the story.

"You apologise," she said. She didn't look angry or even disappointed. "Apologise to both of them. Then you pray to anyone who will listen that they forgive you."

I took a shower and scrubbed my skin until it was pink. Then I sat on the tiles for half an hour, wondering if the water would drown me. I got out after Nora complained through the door that I was the sole cause of the Isle's drought.

I put on clean clothes and lay on my bed, staring at the ceiling until Mum called me down for dinner.

***

School started and trees turned from emerald to gold. I had most of my classes with Joe so I clung to him as much as I could. I managed to avoid Etta and I had no doubt she was going out of her way to avoid me as well.

Joe was focused on trying to get a swimming scholarship, and I was focused on avoiding two very specific people. We both agreed to avoid the volleyball table together.

Cedar Secondary was different when you weren't surrounded by endless gossip at lunch. It was almost bearable.

I noticed that Joni wasn't at school. Not the first week or the second. A month passed and she still didn't show up. Teachers stopped calling her name out in class and new kids eventually filled her seat. It was as if she had never existed at all. I was too scared to ask Joe what had happened.

On the last Friday of September, I finally had my appointment with Ms Meyer. She was a broad woman in her forties with whisky blonde hair and lines around her eyes that deepened when she smiled.

"James," she greeted. "Come in and take a seat."

"It's Jamie," I corrected and walked into her tiny office, which she had decorated with potted plants and photos of people I assumed were her kids.

"Jamie," she reiterated and sat down opposite me. She clicked on her computer and cleared her throat. "Now, I see that you are taking a wide range of subjects. Lots of maths and sciences. Is that a direction you're interested in going towards?"

"My mum wants me to do accounting," I said.

Ms Meyer smiled. "You could definitely do accounting. Your grades are very good. They're also very good in English." She looked up at me again. "Is that something you would be interested in?"

"If it will help me get into accounting."

Ms Meyer clicked her computer screen again and faced me square on. I shuffled in my seat with the gnawing feeling that I was in trouble. "Let's talk about universities. Have you looked into any that might be a good fit for you?"

"It'll be wherever I can get a scholarship."

"Well, most schools offer that."

"Near Cedar then I guess. Although Nora—my sister—says I should go to a city."

Ms Meyer smiled again. "And which one do you want to go to?"

I looked down at my hands. She might as well have been asking me all the other unanswered questions in my head. Why did you kiss Etta when you didn't really like her? Why did you kiss Joni when you went to the dance with Etta? Did you even like either of them or did they both help you run from yourself?

"Jamie?"

"I don't know," I said finally, looking up but unable to meet her eye. "I don't know what to do and I don't know what I like or where I should go."

"That's why I'm here," Ms Meyer said without missing a beat. "How about I send you some courses I think might be a good fit based on your grades. You have an excellent score from advanced biology. We can look at accounting if you'd like and some others. You might do well in an English program. I'll only include the schools with good financial backing."

"Thanks," I mumbled. We arranged another appointment for the next week and she sent me out after the bell went.

Sam was waiting for me in the carpark. "We need to pick up some bits for dinner," she said as I got in.

"My day was great, thanks for asking," I responded sarcastically. Sam ignored me and put the car into drive, joining the queue to get out of the carpark.

"Did you speak to Ms Meyer today?" Sam

asked, drumming her fingers on the steering wheel as we sat at a standstill. The radio was on in the background, the hosts debating the latest fumble made by the Prime Minister.

"You sound like Mum," I grumbled.

Sam stared at me and I could have sworn there was a flicker of hurt across her face. She looked away and said, "Just trying to make conversation but we can sit in silence if you'd prefer."

I opened my mouth to apologise but the words turned to lead in my throat and I said nothing. We drove in silence to the grocery store. When Sam pulled the hand break up she looked over me.

"I'm not going in," I said firmly. I folded my arms across my chest. I knew who could be in there.

"Did you even bother to apologise?" Sam sighed. When I didn't answer she shook her head. "I don't get you at all."

"Mind your own business," I snapped.

Sam froze. She turned to look at me with the exact expression Mum got on her face when she was about to explode with anger. I sank into my seat.

"What's wrong with you?" she began in a more measured voice than I'd expected. "You've moped around the house all September but haven't done anything to make what you did better. You made a mistake but you're not willing to accept the consequences of that." Her words slapped me across my face. Sam wasn't done. "You're going to pick a university based on what Mum wants or Nora wants. You went out with Etta because you knew it made her happy. You went out with Joni because you knew it made *her* happy. Well, what the fuck do you want, *Jamie*? What will make you happy? Because you've tried to please everyone else and look at where you've ended up."

I stared at her, unable to find a response. Sam shook her head and left the car. The door slammed behind her.

What *did* I want?

I dreamt of Joni that night, her hair rippling behind her as we swam in the pool. Her legs wrapped around my waist and then her mouth lowering towards mine—

I woke with a start. Groaning, I turned over and tried to close my eyes. All I could see was her face. My eyes flung open. There was no light behind my blinds and the house was quiet, apart from Nora's snoring echoing through the paper thin walls. I stared at the ceiling and waited for sleep to return.

Minutes or hours might have passed. My mind wandered back to Joni. Instead of her body I thought about how empty the house must be for her. As far as I knew, Ellie hadn't returned, nor her mum who was still staying with Jacky Carson. Nor her dad.

I didn't know much about Leonard Fraser, only that he had been a volleyball star at Cedar Secondary. His name was plastered on every trophy and plaque in the gym.

Joni had left him out of most stories but I recalled them at the grocery store last December, just before he disappeared. They had looked content together; Leonard waiting as Joni selected the apples without bruises and looked over all the eggs in a carton before putting them in the trolley. They had spoken to each other in soft voices, Leonard's face with a wry smile. He didn't look like a man who hated his daughter. Perhaps he had cared so much that he didn't know how to tell her, so he left without a word.

My mind kept wandering, turning these thoughts over and over until sleep captured me again.

Sam planted a seed in my brain that I couldn't stop watering. *What the fuck do you want, Jamie? What do you want?* I didn't know what I wanted.

That was terrifying.

On Sunday morning I read through the courses Ms Meyer sent me. I found a civil engineering course at Willow Park University that was interesting and I could get aid for. There were science courses, too. I printed out the paperwork for various Biology programs and read through them all twice. The English courses intimidated me and I didn't know what I would do with them. But there was something thrilling in that.

I squeezed my eyes shut and tried to picture what I wanted. I just wanted to study something I was interested in and that would give me a fresh start. I circled the courses I was most interested in; some were near Cedar and some were across the country. I could apply for them all and see what landed.

I found Mum in the living room and pressed them into her hands. She looked at them quizzically. "I don't want to do accounting," I told her. "Here are some other options. All have financial aid attached to them."

She stared at me. "Okay," she said.

I blinked. "Okay?"

"Of course, okay. Accounting was just an idea. I want you to be happy." She kissed the top of my head. I was rooted to the spot. "I'll have a read through these."

I was on a high. Mum's reaction to my choice of university had flipped a switch in my brain. I could make a choice and it would be okay for everyone around me. I could make a choice for me.

I decided what I was going to do. I rehearsed it in my head as I showered, going over the lines in front of the bathroom mirror. I changed my shirt three times. Then I put the cardigan in my backpack.

Mum, Nora and Sam were watching a movie so it was easy to sneak past the living room and out the front door. I left a note in Sam's room explaining where I was.

The ride was easy, the evening air fresh as I cycled through the streets of Cedar. I imagined all the ways it might go.

The house was as I remembered it. I walked up the steps and knocked on the door. There was movement behind it and then it swung open and Etta was before me.

"Hi, Etta," I said. I clung onto the cardigan. "May I come in?"

Etta blinked. She had a cherry-coloured jumper and loose black trousers on. The sound of the TV played in the background. Her face was flushed and there was the ghost of a smile on her face. It disappeared as she took me in. I counted the seconds.

"No," said Etta, shaking herself as if she too were waking up.

"Oh—" I hadn't expected such a hard ending. Before I could say anything, Etta stepped outside onto the porch and shut the door.

"You can't come in," she reiterated. "But I will let you talk." She folded her arms across her chest. "Because I'm curious. And because it will be another ridiculous thing you've done that I can laugh about with Skye later."

I deserved that, but it didn't make it any easier to hear. "I want to apologise," I said, trying to keep my voice steady. "I don't think I said it right at the lookout."

"Or the other hundred times you've apologised?" Etta said bluntly.

She wasn't making it easy for me. "I'm an idiot, Etta. But I'm also human and I made a mistake." Before she could launch in, I continued. "It doesn't make it okay but I'm here. I'm trying."

Etta considered this, then said, "Did you even like me?" She fiddled with the ends of her hair.

"You were my best friend," I said because that was the only way I knew how to answer her question.

"But you kissed me," she said after a long silence. Her voice was quiet. It was the first time I had seen her so fragile since the dance.

"I shouldn't have done that," I said. "But I also shouldn't have kissed Joni. I am truly sorry."

Etta bowed her head. "Okay."

I gripped the cardigan. My knuckles turned white. "Maybe one day we could be friends again?"

Etta remained silent, but her breathing had become laboured and when she finally looked up at me I saw that she was crying. I reached out, putting the cardigan between us. Etta took it. I didn't know what to do next; I didn't want to leave again.

"What about Joni?"

I shook my head. "What about Joni?"

"Did you like her—as more than just a friend?"

"I—well—" I rubbed the back of my neck. "I have always liked Joni."

Etta sighed. "You really fucked up, Jamie."

"I know—" I began but Etta put her hand up.

"Joni's gone."

The relatively mild night chilled. I shivered. "I don't understand…What do you mean gone?"

"She left before school started."

"Where is she?" I demanded.

"I don't know," said Etta and there was a hint

of sadness in her tone. "I just know that she isn't in Cedar Valley."

You don't know what you have until it's gone.

I ran back down to my bike and almost fell over as I mounted it.

"Didn't you hear me?" Etta called from the porch.

"I have to try," I said.

"Why?" Etta called. I tried to answer but I couldn't. Etta shook her head. "Thanks for returning my cardigan." Then she closed the door behind her.

I paused, not knowing then that it would be the last time I spoke to her for many years. Then I kicked off the ground and began to cycle.

Skin dripping with chlorine. The consistency and unpredictability of the ocean. Her hair would be damp from taking a shower, smelling like jasmine from her conditioner. She would look at me with shock in her dark eyes, her mouth in a small circle of surprise. *Joni, Joni, Joni.* I rode my bike faster than ever before. I was awake finally, in control of everything. My body felt electric.

The lights were off when I got to Joni's house. Nausea flooded my body and all the hope seeped out.

My bike fell to the ground as I ran to the front door. I rang the bell, then again. I banged my fists against the wood but I knew it was no use. Etta was right. Joni was gone.

I sank to my knees, scrambling for my phone. I dialled her number. The phone rang but it eventually went to voicemail.

"Joni," I breathed, my chest thundering. "It's Jamie. I'm at your house and you're not here and I understand why. I hope you're somewhere nice." I inhaled and then let everything go.

"I think your dad took the photo. The one we spent that afternoon looking for. I think he took it because he still loves you and he cares. He just didn't know how to tell you. Maybe him taking the photo was his way of trying to make you understand." I ran a hand through my hair. "I still care about you, Joni. I don't have anything else to give you other than that. I've fucked up in so many ways but I'm trying to do better now. I just want you to know that I still care."

I stared up at the moon. It shone through behind the clouds. The air was cool against the tears on my cheeks.

"I know your dad left and your sister and your mum. I know I left too—but I came back. I came back for you, Joni. And I really hope that's enough."

Acknowledgements

To
Sidney
Bel
Marta
and Andrew
Thank you for making this book possible.

To
Mum
Katie
Allegra
My friends and family
Anyone who has read my books
Thank you for caring.

And to Jeff
Thank you for chasing the gloomy days away.

About the Author

Abbie Amy is a writer, poet and storyteller based in London. She has written and published two books of poetry, *Ink for Two* and *Daughter of Wednesday*.

Heatwave is her first novella.

You can find her on Instagram @booksbyabbie.